Willa's Love

Jewel Adams

Published by Jewel Adams, 2024.

WILLA'S LOVE

First edition. November 24, 2024.

Copyright © 2024 Jewel Adams.

ISBN: 979-8227468123

Written by Jewel Adams.

Table of Contents

Willa's Love

CHAPTER ONE

Willa held her hands up to the fire, sighing over the warmth floating across her icy fingertips. "Hmm, much better." She reached for another log and tossed it on the glowing red coals. "That should hold it for a while."

A frown marred her brow as she looked again at the snow blowing past the cabin's window. Without thought, she pulled the shawl closer, wishing it were thicker to ward off the cold that captured her. "How did I get here? And in a stupid blizzard no less."

No answer came from the silent cabin. There was no one to answer all the questions she asked these last days. Willamena shivered over where she still found herself. "How, darn it?"

All the reasons she could think of didn't lend any answers. No, only questions raced through her mind over how or why she came to be standing in a place she feared was a long way from home. Her gaze raced about the cabin that looked ancient even though it wasn't. "Amnesia? But then, why do I remember who I am and where I'm supposed to be living? This certainly isn't my apartment."

Who the place belonged to remained a mystery, "Calvin," the name filled her with a familiar feeling. "Is this place yours?" It became the one answer she worried over more than the others.

She looked again at the long-barreled gun that should be in a museum, not hanging over the fireplace. By the door, a man's pair of boots stood beneath a huge fur coat that she could get lost in. Willa wasn't anxious to meet the man who wore them or used the gun. Where he might be remained as large a mystery as how she came to be in his home. Something told her he wouldn't be happy to find her camped out in front of his hearth. "Well, my fire, his wood," she looked around. "His house?"

Releasing her pent-up breath, she wanted to scream again, but her throat felt raw from her last screaming fit. "Not that it helped."

Wherever she was, Willa decided there weren't any people around. "No, they would have come running to see who was dying." Her fear-filled screams sounded as if someone were killing her. Only, no one touched her and yet someone must have put her here. *Or something?* She pushed away the unlikable thought.

Once again, the vision filled her memory. She'd just arrived home from work and put the grocery bag on the breakfast bar. Odd how she remembered the crazy feeling that filled her, "as if I were weightless..." then nothing, only a suffocating darkness that swallowed her in its depths.

It took a moment for her to open her eyes, wishing beyond hope she'd find herself back at her house. Willa bit her lip as the rustic cabin stole away the hope she refused to let leave her. Three days, yes, that is how long it had been since she woke up here. "Well, the morning of the fourth day."

Shortening the time didn't change where she found herself. The first day, she'd sat in the corner, shivering, crying, and then screaming in anger and fear—demanding to be taken back!

How long she cried in numb denial, she couldn't remember. Not doing something to help herself went beyond Willa's capabilities. Yesterday, she explored the small two-room cabin; she refused to feel guilty over going through all his drawers. If nothing else, Willa only found evidence that a man lived there.

Her fingers closed over the dress's material she found in the trunk in his closet. "A woman once lived here..."

The letter she read confirmed her feelings and the death of his wife...Ruth. "Calvin's wife."

The name came like a whisper across her lips. His entry in the family bible didn't need any explanation—*Ruth Ann Masterson, wife of Calvin Paul Masterson, died in childbirth on November 22, 1883...she was loved and will be missed beyond thought.*

His words hadn't left her since she read them. Her lips trembled, "Three years ago..." The newspaper she found in the kindling box told her that much. What it didn't tell her is how she, a woman from over a hundred years in the future, came to be here in Calvin Masterson's home in 1886.

Willa shook off the terror the facts created. She already wasted three days, "shock, that's what I feel, but enough!"

She pushed off the floor and forced herself to walk into the small kitchen area. There weren't that many things on the shelf by the window. Willa pulled down the bread tins and a jar of bacon grease. She told herself she needed food, but more, she needed to do something normal. "Bread…" She opened the one crock she found and sniffed, pulling back from the yeast's pungent odor. The large bowl came next as she gathered all the supplies she found. Willa looked at the door and wished she'd been brave enough to go outside, wondering if she would have found chickens and maybe some eggs.

She lacked things like milk and eggs to make the bread, but once she found oats, Willa's tight lips eased in a small smile. "I know how to make oatmeal bread."

Grain bread was not new to her, and Willa felt relieved she could use what was on hand to make something as she mixed up the oatmeal for bread.

The wind howled outside. She refused to look. The storm that started during the night seemed to worsen, and Willamena couldn't help but worry over the missing Calvin Masterson. Her teeth raked across her bottom lip as she worked. The chore couldn't outweigh her conviction that the man was out in the blizzard.

"The coals I found say he was here before I arrived." She pushed her hands to whip the batter and pour it into the bread tins. "They were still warm. He couldn't have been gone too long."

As she closed the oven door at the side of the fireplace, Willa faced her fears for the man she expected to confront before now. She didn't want to face the man's anger over finding a stranger in his home. Explaining her presence wouldn't be easy when she didn't know how she got here. "He probably won't give me a chance even to try and explain."

She pulled the last log from the wood box to put on the fire. Her hand shook over the truth that she needed to go outside and get more wood.

Willa took a deep breath before walking to the door. "I hope he is an understanding man."

She reached for the fur coat and put her arm into the sleeve. A nervous giggle passed her lips over the distance left in the sleeve she didn't fill. Willa worked to roll up the sleeves. She found gloves in the pocket but gave up trying to wear them; their size was just too large, as were the boots. "I don't have much choice."

Determined, she shoved her foot into the large boot. Before going outside, she took a few steps, sliding her foot forward to keep the boots on. The coat's belt at least kept it around her. With more courage than she felt, she pulled the wooden peg out of the latch and opened the door.

The blast of frigid air engulfed her as she fought to reclose the door, not wanting to lose any of the warmth inside the cabin. Willa looked around her, trying to see through the blowing snow where the wood might be. She finally saw the wood stacked to the left of the house and moved slowly through the snow. Thankfully, the boots stayed on her feet.

She gathered as many logs as she could carry to the door and dropped them there to go back for more. After four trips, Willa decided she had enough to last the day and night as she worked to carry them inside the house.

Willa opened the door for the last load of wood only to catch her breath over the large form moving towards her. When the shape fell forward, Willa dropped the wood, snapped out her shock, and rushed to help. She pulled and pulled on the man's arm, "Come on, it is only a short way more!"

She took hold of him and dragged him with her. Yelling at him to move didn't seem to help much, but she finally managed to get him inside the house.

Willa pulled him in enough to shut the door and drag him to the fire. She couldn't do more than let him lie in front of the hearth. She shrugged out of the coat and kicked away the boots to help him. "Calvin?" She frowned as she worked to get the ice-caked coat off of him. "It must be you. Please don't die. I need you more than you know."

Feeling foolish for talking to the unconscious man, Willa kept working. Finally, getting the coat off, she went to remove his boots and confronted the snowshoes. She struggled with the knots holding them onto the shoes, nearly crying in frustration when they refused to loosen. Rushing to the kitchen, she came back with the knife and sawed through the rawhide cords, wanting to shout when the last knot let go.

The man's pants were soaked to his skin, and so were his socks. Willa only hesitated for a moment before stripping off the wet, icy clothing. She knew she needed to get him warm before he died from exposure. His body looked blue from the cold, and she could see the shivers rolling over him. "He's been out in this forever!"

She worked like a woman possessed, refusing to stop until she managed to get all his clothing off. She threw logs onto the fire and pulled the bread before it burned as she rushed back to him.

He was so big and heavy, "dead weight, bad choice of words, Willamena." She fought to get his long legs and body under the quilts she pulled off the bed. She remembered the corn in one crock. Willa went to the drawer she knew held his socks and pulled out the dry pairs. She filled them with corn kernels and placed them inside a big iron kettle. Willa huffed and worked to get the kettle on the hook over the fire; once on, she pushed the kettle as close to the fire as she dared to heat the kernels. "If only it were rice, we don't need popcorn." She prayed the corn would get warm enough before popping to place the socks around him for warmth.

She couldn't remember how long she worked to get the man, whom she hoped was Calvin Masterson, surrounded by heat from the corn-filled socks. As she settled the last filled sock about his feet, she pulled the covers up and under his chin before tucking them in. "There, it should help."

Her hand reached out, and Willa moved the dark lock of hair away from his forehead. She blushed over the vivid images she held of his magnificent body. "Hmm, even with the beard, you are a handsome man, Calvin Masterson."

. . ⟨⟩ . .

Willa lost track of how long she tended to Calvin. His incoherent ramblings seemed to be getting worse. She took the warm cloth and wiped the sweat from his face. Her palm pulled back from his brow over the heat coming from him. "A fever...no!"

Willa inwardly groaned, knowing there wasn't any drugstore or doctor to call for medicine, and she didn't remember finding anything that even resembled medicine in her search of the place. "I remember my grandmother saying you have to sweat out the fever...I wonder."

More logs went on the fire. She made a broth from the oatmeal for him, hoping he would take some. She held his head up against her breasts and pressed the warm cup against his lips, sighing when he managed to drink some. "A little more, please, Calvin; drink more. It is nice and warm."

But the man was beyond hearing her. Willa gave up and carefully moved his head back to the pillows. Her hand slipped under the covers to check the warmth from the socks lining his body. She blushed again, remembering how fine a body he possessed.

"I'm not very good with timing, am I?" She frowned as she tucked the blankets back around him, "Time, that's what this is. Have I come through time..." She looked at him, "to save you?" Had she? Was she here to save this man? "How crazy is that for an answer over what has happened to me?" She looked at the man again, "I don't think you will like that as an explanation for having a stranger invade your home."

Willa put all her efforts into taking care of the man, not realizing it was dark, until she went to retrieve more wood, fearing she might run out during the night. The storm seemed to be getting worse as she listened to the howling wind. The man's groans sounded as bad as the wind.

The cooling cloth she wiped over him did little to help cool his fever, but when he suddenly went into chills, Willa's concern deepened. "Calvin, you need to fight this."

Willa wanted to groan with him as his entire body became gripped in the chill ravaging his body. She wasn't sure what to do for him. She put every blanket she could find over him, knowing it would take too long to heat the socks again. Her decision was made. "I sure hope you don't remember any of this."

Her clothes quickly ended up in a pool at her feet. She lifted the covers and brushed away the last of her indecision as she moved in beside him. Willa pulled him close to her naked body, holding him to give the man the heat from her own. When, at last, he began to settle down, she wanted to groan over the hold his muscled arms captured her in. The man's head came to rest between her breasts, and Willa bit her lips not to respond to the feelings he created. The way his legs weaved around her own made her groan. That she could feel every glorious muscle of his awesome frame didn't help her much. "I guess feeling a man—such large a man, against me—on me—for the first time ranks right up there with time travel." Talking to herself became another new experience, "guess I should have expected this too."

Willa couldn't remember how many hours she used soothing strokes and words to calm his fevered thrashing. She tried many times to move out from under him, but each time, his hold would tighten to keep her in place. Her exhaustion finally ruled as his body's temperature came down. "Sleep, Calvin, just sleep..." Her finger wove into the lush thickness of his hair as he snuggled closer. Her fingers slowly stilled as sleep overtook her in his arms.

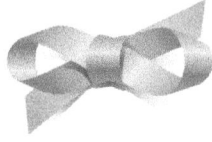

CHAPTER 2

Calvin's arm tightened about the soft, feminine body molded against him. He'd long given up the idea the woman was another dream. No, dreams didn't feel like this; they didn't make him desire things lost in his life for more years than he wanted to remember.

She felt so small beneath his hand as his palm traveled over the satiny curves of her naked body. He looked again about the cabin to confirm he was inside his own home—and that they were together in *his* bed. Where the woman came from, he couldn't imagine. That she probably saved his life, he didn't doubt. He held vivid memories of her beautiful face and that angel voice talking to him, nursing his fevered body. He remembered seeing her moving about the cabin, bringing in wood for the fire...

His fingers moved through the silky softness of her long blonde hair. Calvin couldn't remember feeling anything this soft since...no, he refused to think about her.

Every delicate inch of the woman was imprinted on his senses. She started waking up, and his hold instinctively tightened to keep her exactly where she lay. He wanted to cherish the bold warmth of her silken, warm muff pressed against his thick thigh. It took all his control not to pull her over the evidence of his growing desire. She couldn't stand higher than his shoulder, but she was all woman. Calvin swallowed hard over the way her ample breasts pressed against his chest. Their lush fullness molded with his hot flesh in wanton pleasure. He could even feel the taut nubs of her round globes. The weighted pleasure of her breasts would fill his palms.

Unable to stop himself, Calvin let his hand move to touch the side of her breast. *Like velvet...* He felt her body tense; the truth that he didn't want to stop with just a touch fired his loins.

The man moved faster than she could, and Willa froze as the full length of his extraordinary body pressed down upon her...naked body!

Willa felt the heat flooding her cheeks, refusing to open her eyes. She failed to move away. She needed to get up and stoke the fire. Willa swallowed hard over the truth that she didn't want to destroy the feelings every brazen inch of his body created. Every capturing touch of the man seemed to become a permanent part of her. The bold muscles of his thighs locked her in place, burning his imprint to her very soul. It was an erotic power she wanted to explore beyond all other thoughts.

Calvin waited for her beautiful eyes to open, wanting to see what color they held. His fingers moved back the solid wave of silken hair from her face. When she finally lost the battle she waged with herself, the bright green light of her gaze seemed to capture his own—pulling him into their open depths. If he expected fear, she failed to show any; curiosity is what filled those forestry beauties. That his manhood pressed against her furred, womanly heat only enhanced the woman's appeal. He knew she couldn't move without becoming more intimate.

"You slept with me."

"You are awake."

Calvin couldn't help but smile over the wonderment in her sweet voice. "I am better."

"You still feel feverish." She couldn't escape the heat of his flesh. Willa wanted to pull away from his devouring gaze. When she managed to gain her freedom, her gaze seemed determined to fail her as it fell to his lips.

Calvin felt the fire strike through him over the way her delicate tongue came out and rolled over her lips. He lowered his to answer her silent request, glorying in the opening invitation.

Gentle yet firm, his mouth covered hers, his tongue demanded entrance, and Willa had no power to refuse him. Devour was mild for his claiming kiss, and she opened dear heavens. She did open for him. She wanted to feel it all, allowing him to discover all he sought. Willa leaned into the warmth of his large palm as it cupped the side of her head, and she arched her neck as his lips sought more, explored more as they moved down her neck...

He felt the instant change wash over her when his kiss whisked over the top of her breast. Calvin groaned over the douse of reality he suspected took hold of the lady. He pulled slowly back, taking small but vital kisses as he worked his way back to her lips, ones he recaptured and relished in all their heated excitement.

Willa sucked in her breath once he finally pulled away, causing her to groan over the loss. "Calvin..." His name rushed past her swollen lips, and she wished he would come back.

"You know more of me than I of you."

Her eyes opened to confront the anger she heard and felt coursing through his powerful body. She wondered where the gentleness went, regretting the dark, closed look now staring at her. "Willa...Willamena Garrison."

His brow arched, and she wanted to slide away, but his hold on her prevented her from escaping. The time she dreaded was here, and Willa wondered if she would end up in the snow outside. "Would you like some tea? I made bread if you are hungry..."

Calvin hid his mirth over her nervous rambling, wondering how this beauty did come to his house. "You have been in my home for a while, I take it."

He watched her teeth jut out to catch her bottom lip, still swelled from his kiss. She was nervous, but he knew he was the cause. Calvin decided to keep hold of her until she answered all his questions. "I think you should explain yourself, Willamena."

The way he said her name made her cock her head to the side. She ran her tongue over her lip and sucked in her breath over the taste of him still lingering there.

"You aren't paying attention, Willa."

She rolled her eyes and wished he wasn't lying on top of her, "You make it hard to concentrate, Calvin."

She proved more honest than he expected. "How do you know my name?"

"This is your house."

He tightened his hold on her arms, "And you are in it. Why?" He didn't miss the worry his question caused her. "It would be best to tell me the truth."

"I'm trying to do that...only, I don't know."

"You don't know what?"

Willa knew she exasperated him. "I don't know how I got here."

She suffered his scrutiny, and he didn't hide any of his anger from her.

"That's it—that is your answer?"

"I'm afraid so, Calvin."

"How do you know my name?"

"The Bible." She answered softly.

Calvin shook her over the answer. Realizing what he did, he stilled his hands and took a deep breath to quell his anger. "You read my bible?"

"Yes, I'm sorry." Willa knew she was only making him angrier. "I needed to find out where I was...I snooped through your house, I..."

"Stop!" Calvin's breath came hard and fast. Every move she made seemed to penetrate his body and divert his attention. "You make no sense. Who brought you out here?"

"I don't know, honest, Calvin. I just don't know."

He decided she was either as scared as she looked or a very good liar.

"You want me to believe you don't know how you came to be in my home, lying with me..."

"No, I know how I—you were having violent chills, and the socks would have taken too long to reheat..."

"Socks?"

She nodded and smiled, "Yes, the socks, well, the corn heats up to get you warm. You were very cold and had a fever, then chills. I couldn't heat the corn again, and you needed heat, so I got undressed and..." Calvin's head dropped to her chest, "Calvin?"

She didn't breathe as she watched his head slowly rise. His eyes looked so dark she wanted to hide.

"You are unbelievable."

"I'm telling you the truth. I know it isn't much, but I did try to help."

"By getting naked and coming into my bed..."

"Yes, that's right, Calvin." Her hand reached up and pushed back the stubborn lock of his hair that fell over his brow. Her palm rested over his brow. "You may be better, but you still feel hot."

Calvin took hold of her wrist and, pulled her hand down beside her head and held it there. "Enough! Do you have any idea what you have done?"

"Helped break your fever?" Something told Willa she was in more trouble than she expected. "Calvin?"

"You are in my bed, Willamena, my bed..."

She swallowed the thought to correct him. The floor wasn't exactly his bed. "Yes, you needed the warmth of my..."

His finger covered her lips, "Hush, just hush." Calvin stared at her and wondered if she was addled. He heard of people who lost their minds up here; the loneliness drove them crazy. Was she one of these people?

The deep breath he took for control proved a huge mistake when her essence swept through him. Her sensual scent penetrated every pore of his body, and Calvin admitted he wanted her. Sanity came hard as his reality struck hard and fierce. No woman had been in this cabin. To be in his bed, with him, naked...he reeled over the implications.

"I'm very tired, Willamena, and I need to think about this, about you."

Calvin forced himself to move off her and let her go. He watched as she gathered one of the quilts around her, covering every beautiful part of her exquisite body. Except when she turned, the quilt fell down her lovely back to her buttocks. He could see where her hips flared from her waist. "Beautiful..."

Willa stopped herself from turning. She couldn't help but smile over his husky compliment. "Get some rest, Calvin."

"That will not be easy, Willa."

"Do you have any chickens?"

"Hmm? Chickens? Yes, in the barn."

The way his voice faded, she knew he had fallen asleep. She slid off the bed, keeping the blanket around her as she turned and looked upon the man. "You're pretty darn handsome, yourself, Calvin Masterson."

For a second, Willa allowed all the feelings he created to rush through her. She swayed under her body's wanton response. "Darn, awesome."

Willa sighed and tried to gather her thoughts. "Of course, I've no one to compare you to."

She brushed the thought away and set her mind on finding the chickens. "Poor things haven't been fed for days." Willa gasped, "What if there are more animals? Oh dear, I need to find out."

As she bent to retrieve the discarded clothes, she couldn't help but look at him again. His warmth still clung to her, she wished it would stay, and she smiled over the admission. "So many changes, so quickly, it's a wonder I'm not a basket case."

Willa looked around and realized there was no place in the cabin that offered any privacy. She studied him, watching to make sure he was asleep. After watching his chest rise and fall in perfect rhythm, Willa let the quilt drop and hurried to dress. She quickly rekindled the fire, ensuring the log caught before leaving it.

Once the coat and boots were back on, she took a deep breath and opened the door. To her surprise, the wind no longer blew like a torrent. "A winter wonderland, wow, it is beautiful." The snow sparkled under the sun. She didn't feel the cold over the beauty surrounding her. Without the whirling snow she quickly located the barn, amazed that it stood so close and she couldn't see it before.

Making her way to the barn took more effort than she expected. Willa kept losing the boots. The snow sucked them off. When she reached the barn, she needed to stop and catch her breath before opening the door. Thankfully, the smaller door she saw opened for her once she cleared away the snow. The barn felt warmer than outside. When her eyes adjusted to the shadowed light, she felt her lips easy into a smile. "Ahh, hello, everyone. My goodness." She stood there as the various heads poked themselves out of the stalls. Chickens walked around her as if inspecting the new visitor. "Guess I better figure out how to feed you all."

Willa opened bins and found grain she felt the cow and horse could use. There was also hay; she put armfuls into each stall. She threw down cracked corn for the hens, laughing over the way they pecked at each piece. "I wonder where the eggs might be."

She watched the hens, realizing they had little cubbies built into the wall at the back of the barn. "I hope these don't have chicks in them." Willa found a basket and placed about a dozen eggs in it to take back to the house.

The cow let out an awful moo, making her jump in surprise. "Goodness, what was that for?"

Willa moved back to the stall where the cow stood and watched the animal kick at the floor as if irritated. "What's wrong, lady?"

The huge sac of milk under the cow gave Willa her answer. She chewed her lip, trying to decide what to do about the cow. A small stool and pail sat outside the stall. Taking a deep breath, she let it out in a rush. "What the heck. I might as well try. Milking a cow is mild compared to time travel and—Calvin." She fought back the rush of heat attacking her body over the thought of him. She made herself focus on what needed to be done. "Just don't kick me, okay?"

She gathered up the stool and pail and set both beside the cow where she thought best. Willa took her seat on the stool and patted the cow when its large head turned to look at her. "Okay, I'm getting there. Just relax."

The nipples felt like warm velvet in her hands. She pulled them down, but nothing happened. Repositioning her hands, she tried again with more of a massage-type pull. A stream of hot milk hit the ground. Her laughter filled the barn, "now that is unreal."

After a few more tries, she managed to hit the pail. Willa rested the side of her head against the warm belly of the cow as she continued to work each nipple. It seemed like an hour passed before she finished with nearly a full pail. "My goodness, you needed to be milked. I'll try not to make you wait..." Would there be a next time? Willa pushed the troubling thought away. For now, he needed her. "A day at a time...time, guess there's no way to control it."

CHAPTER 3

Calvin watched her through half-closed eyes. He nearly panicked when he woke, and she wasn't there; then he heard her laughter coming from outside. He cursed the weakness that kept him from discovering what she was up to. Seeing the pail of milk and basket of eggs, he figured she found the barn.

He probably should have told her he was awake, but Calvin couldn't stop watching her. She looked so pleased with herself as she moved about the kitchen humming. He saw her pick up one of the eggs and smile at it as if it were some marvelous invention. His curiosity mounted concerning his little visitor. Earlier, when he started to tell her about being in his bed, she seemed oblivious to the consequences. Calvin wondered if she could truly be that naïve. Was she a virgin?

The thought tore through his body, weakening him under the assault. Mixed feelings swirled through his thoughts. All the questions were answered if she were.

She was talking to herself, and Calvin forced himself to listen.

"...real, untouched milk. Well, I did sort of touch it." The wonder floated through the room in a soft laugh. "I actually milked a cow!"

Everything seemed so new to her as if she had never done these common chores before. Calvin wondered what kind of upbringing she had that lacked such basic tasks. The puzzle that came with the beauty seemed to be getting bigger. He wished he felt better, but confronting her now wouldn't work. Calvin felt he would need all his wits about him where Willamena was concerned. Inwardly, he smiled. She may be new to this type of life, but the lady thoroughly enjoyed her discoveries.

She captured his attention as he watched her gather up bowls and supplies. The way she stilled, her teeth worked over her bottom lip. She did that before, and he decided she did it deep in thought, like now. He watched as she looked over everything, and then, as if coming to a decision, she began measuring out the milk and flour.

Calvin's eyelids grew heavy, but he fought to go to sleep; watching her gave him a sense of peace, something he hadn't felt for a very long time.

Willa chanced another look across the room. "He's finally asleep."

She smiled, wondering how long he watched her before she realized he wasn't asleep. "You certainly have my attention, Calvin Masterson."

The egg almost slipped out of her hand over the memory of how his body felt against her bare flesh. "My goodness, I think I've been missing a lot by not dating Calvin." She worked on making up the polenta, hoping he would like it. At least she had eggs and bread to go with it. The apple cake she made up should get him to eat. She would take the peels to the horse, smiling over her discovery of the apples in the barn.

She looked again at him. He wasn't as well as he thought. No, a healthy man didn't sleep through the day. "Wood, I better get some more in here."

After working on finishing the polenta, Willa struggled with the coat and boots.

After five loads of wood and two more stacked up by the steps under the overhang, Willa felt good about the supply. If he did take to a chill again, the wood would need to be enough. "I don't think I can take another night in your arms." She sucked in her breath over the vivid memory. "No, I'd want a heck of a lot more than touching..."

"What's the matter, Willa? You didn't protest much."

She gasped and spun about to face Calvin. "Calvin..."

Her surprise vanished over watching him struggle to sit up in bed.

"Here, let me help." Willa slipped her arm under his to help him sit up.

But when he didn't move, she finally turned to look at him. His breath brushed her lips. "Don't you want to sit up?" She managed to voice the question.

"You are a danger, Willa." His gaze searched her lovely face and the eyes that stared at him in wonder. "Do you always want strangers to kiss you?"

Willa would have pulled back over his question, but his arms came around her and held her in place. Somehow, she knew he wouldn't release her until she answered. "No, Calvin, you are the only man I've ever wanted to kiss me."

"Honesty, Willa?"

"The truth, Calvin, just the truth." When she pulled back, he let her go. Willa straightened up in slow caution, smoothing down the front of the dress. "I'll have dinner ready for you very soon."

She moved to leave him, then turned back. "Seriously, do you need help getting up?"

He never stopped studying her, "No, I'm fine." Calvin's tight gaze followed her every step, still wondering about her answer. "Where are you from, Willamena?"

She refused to break her concentration on fixing him a meal. "Boston."

"That's a far distance from Idaho."

"You have no idea just how far, Calvin."

"Maybe you ought to tell me, Willa?" It took all his control to keep his anger under control. He wanted answers from this lady, one that seemed to fill even his dreams.

Willa kept moving, knowing he was watching her. "Let me fix your dinner, then I will try to answer."

"Alright, Willa, but my patience is about gone."

He caught the slight smile that passed over her before she answered.

"No doubt." Willa pulled off the apron and went to the table.

Calvin started to object when she held up her hand to stop him. She worked at dragging over the table to the bed. "You aren't up to getting out of bed yet."

She moved back to gather up the dishes and bring them over to him. "It isn't much, but it should help get your energy back. She reached over the table and placed her palm over his forehead. "You still have a fever. Try to eat."

Calvin waited for her to place the last dish on the table. "Where is your plate, Willa?"

"I'm not..."

He set his silverware down and looked at her in meaning.

"Calvin?"

"I won't eat alone. I've done that enough."

She gave him a slight nod of assent and went back into the kitchen to get her place setting.

Neither of them spoke as they filled their plates. Calvin put more food on her plate when the amount he saw earned his *humph*.

Calvin waited on his questions until he felt she'd eaten about all she could force down. His plate was clean, and he enjoyed her meal. "How far is it, Willa?"

Willa's fork halted in midair over his question. She slowly put the filled fork down on her plate. "Calvin, I don't know how I came to be in your home. I...well, I was just here."

The incredulous stare he held her in made her fidget. "It's true, I was home and then—here, that happened four days ago."

"Willa..."

She pushed away from the table, "No, don't say it. I know it sounds crazy. Heck, I felt crazy, but it happened, and I don't know how. I just don't know."

Calvin watched her spin about when her pacing took her to the door. He knew if she tried to go out, he would have stopped her. "Can you sit back down? You are making me dizzy."

She stopped, her hands on her hips, and Calvin couldn't remember seeing a more beautiful, angry woman.

"It's the truth, Calvin. I'm not lying. I just found myself here!"

He could see how angry and upset the admission made her. "What about your family?"

"Family? I don't have any."

No family? He wondered how a warm, giving woman could be without a family. Calvin had to know. "What about a husband, Willa?"

She stopped pacing and looked at him. "I'm not married, Calvin. I haven't even dated." His questioning look told her how ridiculous he felt her answer was. "Calvin, what year is this?"

"The date?"

She nodded in answer.

"It would be November 18th, 1887." Calvin schooled himself not to show her how much her question worried him. Watching her pale before him only made his feelings concerning her worsen. "What was the date you left your home, Willamena?"

For a second, the confusion on her face made him wonder if she even knew; her answer only caused his disbelief.

"April 2, 2010, Calvin. I'm from the year 2010, not 1887." Willa brushed away the tears from her cheeks, knowing how crazy she must sound to this man. "It is the truth, Calvin. Somehow, I came here to your home, and I have no idea how it happened."

He started to say something, and she held up her hand. "No, I realize it sounds crazy, but I'm not! It happened, and that is all I can tell you."

Calvin sat there watching her putting on his fur coat and slip those tiny feet into his large boots and couldn't think of anything to say.

She couldn't look at him, fearing what she would see. "I need to milk the cow and gather the eggs. I'll feed them, too."

The door slammed behind her leave.

His breath rushed out, "You are right—it is crazy."

·· ❧ ··

She paced the length of the barn again, and still, she found no release from the fear gripping her. "It is the truth, darn it all! I don't lie, and I would never make this up."

Calvin resisted telling her he was there, too involved in watching the glorious vision she made. That he'd been watching her for quite some time wouldn't set well with the woman. The fact he heard all her arguments over how she got here and why, struck him hard. No, he didn't believe she lied, didn't from the first. No one would make up a story this farfetched.

He shook his head, deciding they both needed to get back inside. Calvin pushed off the wall and out of the shadow that hid his presence from her. "Willa..."

"Oh! Calvin, oh no, you shouldn't be out here. You aren't well."

When she came at him he knew to push him back toward the cabin, Calvin pulled her up against him. "Hush, Willa, just hush and calm down. It's alright, honey, calm down."

Willa slowly stopped her struggle. Closing her eyes, she let his large hand press her cheek against his chest as his fingers moved through her hair. "I..."

"Shh, you've worked yourself into a fine state, Willa." Calvin felt her tremble beneath his touch. His chin came to rest on the top of her head. "It will be alright."

Willa took a couple of steady breaths. "Will it, Calvin? Will it ever be alright?"

"Sure, it will, honey. You have to let yourself breathe."

She pushed back and looked up into his dark blue eyes. "It did happen..."

His finger stopped her from saying it again. "I know, I believe you."

She pulled his hand down, "You do? Honest?"

Calvin smiled at her, "I believe you."

Willa leaned her head sideways and studied him. "You don't believe it happened, do you?"

His head shook, "I believe you do though. But, Willa, what you are saying, well it isn't believable."

She sighed, "I know. I wish I had some proof."

"You don't."

It was her turn to shake her head no.

"So why don't we both accept this part of you and move on to the next problem."

"Problem? What kind of problem, Calvin?" Willa could hear the shaking in her voice.

He wondered if waiting would be better then gave up the thought. "You are here, in my house Willa."

"Yes, I'm sorry, I..."

"Hush, sweet lady, you need to hush and listen to me for a change." He waited for her to nod her agreement to listen. "We spent the night together—in my bed."

"Calvin, I know that, but you needed..."

He silenced her the only way possible, and Calvin pushed his advantage, deepening the kiss until he felt her weaken against his frame. Ever so slowly he pulled back, hating to stop what he started. "Like I said, you were in my bed, Willa. Where I come from, that only means one thing."

The question that came over her nearly defeated him. "Willa—we will go to the town as soon as possible, and the reverend will perform the marriage..."

She pulled back out of his arms, and Calvin felt himself tense over the fight he hoped to avoid. No, Willa wasn't like any woman he knew. There wasn't a lady anywhere who wouldn't insist on marriage. Somehow, he never expected her to accept his decree, but then Calvin wasn't asking.

"Willa?"

Her hand came up, "No, you stay right there, Calvin Masterson!" She stepped back when he moved forward. "Where did marriage come from? I don't want to marry anyone."

"You will marry me, Willamena Garrison. Just as soon as I can make it happen."

"Oh no, I won't!" And she thought she was the crazy one. "I was only giving you the heat you needed."

"I think you probably saved my life."

She nodded as she took another step back. "Probably, but I didn't expect marriage in return."

"Get'n it anyways."

CHAPTER 4

Calvin steadied the thick piece of wood on the stump. Something else crashed against the cabin wall, and Calvin wondered if the place would survive her tirade. He smiled and brought his ax down, splitting the log.

Picking up another piece, "She isn't like any woman I know. But the lady's temper is glorious!" His ax split another log.

When the cabin door opened, he kept working on the wood, but his attention was on the lady. She looked like she could take on a bear, making him wonder if the eggs would arrive in one piece. He wouldn't be surprised if a few didn't end up splattered against the barn wall. He shook his head, and the ax came down, splitting the log. As he bent to pick the pieces up, he caught her struggles with his boots.

He'd pulled out the traveling bag that held Ruth's clothing. Calvin worried about seeing them again, but for some odd reason, on Willa, nothing looked familiar. She is a beautiful woman, and the tightness of the garments attested to the fact that she possessed more curves and that her breasts were fuller. "Stubborn, too."

Another swing of the ax split the log. She'd slept on the floor in front of the fire last night, refusing to get into bed with him. Calvin didn't get much rest worrying about her. He refused to admit he missed having her beside him, but the truth wouldn't be dismissed. Out of self-preservation she would sleep in the bed tonight.

His gaze went up to the heavy clouds that promised more snow. Their darkness said it would be a blow like that last one.

Calvin started gathering the wood. He filled the area by the door that Willa set up and went back for more to fill the box inside. The livestock needed to be tended to.

The barn was dark, and he could hear Willa singing. Calvin walked in to check the stalls only to find that she already fed the horse and cow; by the soft murmurs of the chickens, they, too, were fine. It seemed she liked tending to the animals. He moved closer to see what she was singing about.

Calvin saw her head resting against the cow's stomach as she milked her. The song wasn't one he knew, but he liked the soft melody. He didn't want to disturb her and started to back away.

"I haven't fetched the eggs yet, Calvin, if you don't mind." Willa didn't change her position, but her gaze followed him as he took the basket and went to the coop at the back of the barn.

Willa swallowed her temper; they needed to talk, and being angry wouldn't accomplish anything. She realized her modern-day values didn't come close to his. "Puritan? No, probably outdated would be better."

"Did you say something, Willa?"

She hid her smile against the cow, "No, just talking to myself. There, that's the last of the milk."

Calvin reached around her and lifted the full bucket. "Could you take the eggs?"

"Sure." Willa took the basket from his hand.

"I want to grab the ham. There is another storm blowing in."

He watched her eyes grow larger.

"Really? My goodness, is this usual for here?"

"No, the last storm came out of nowhere. We had a very wet summer as well. The crops did good, though."

She walked beside him, "That's why you were caught out in it.

"Yes."

"I saw all the corn and hay you put up."

"It should last the winter, better than the year before."

She walked through the door he held open for her. "I fed all the livestock and gave them hay. Do I need to give them extra?"

Calvin smiled down at her; her head came under his arm as he held the door. "I'll tie up a rope to find my way to the barn during the storm. They will be fine for a day if need be."

She was going to say she could do it but snapped her mouth shut.

"I am glad you like working with the animals, Willa. With you feeding and milking, I can put my time into other projects."

She stopped and stared up at him, wondering if he read minds or something. "I don't mind taking care of them."

There she said it, she nervously returned his smile. Willa wondered why he wasn't angry with her. She would be upset if someone just happened to be in her house.

"Will you be alright carving off some meat from the ham, or would you like me to, Willa?"

She shut the door behind him, glad to be inside in the heat. She caught the quick look around he made, and she nearly laughed, knowing that he expected a mess. Willa could feel the blush creeping over her, knowing she acted poorly. The man's home was invaded. He should be the one to be angry.

"Willa?"

"Could you please do it." She moved past him at the work area to begin dinner. A deep breath didn't take the worry away. His insistence that they would get married still needed to be discussed.

He watched her smell the milk as if it were a heavenly aroma. "You like milk that much?"

Her cheeks flamed over being caught. She couldn't help it; the milk, eggs, everything was new. "I've never milked a cow or gathered eggs before. I enjoy it very much."

"Wait until you try making butter." Calvin stopped sharpening the knife. Her cheeks were high in color, and she looked beautiful. "How did you get these things?"

Willa decided she might as well try to explain things to Calvin. "Where I come from, these items are in neat packages, and you go to the store to get them."

"It must be a large town for people to buy from stores."

She studied him for a minute and wondered how he would take her words. "Things are very different. People don't raise their food like here. I find your way has many more benefits than just the food."

He could tell by the tone of her voice that she was back to talking about the future. "I don't think I would like your time, Willa."

Did he mean he believed her? No, she could see his cautious look upon her and knew he just said that so she wouldn't get angry again. "No, Calvin, no, you wouldn't."

She turned away from him, and Calvin wanted to take hold of her shoulders and make her look at him. His grip tightened about the knife not to touch her.

. . ✿ . .

"It isn't a good idea, Calvin."

"You need to get into the bed, Willa. It is too cold to be on the floor."

She glared at him, and Calvin wanted nothing more than to pull her to him and hold her. He knew she was right. They shouldn't sleep together, but neither could he let her sleep on the floor another night.

"Come on, Willa, I need your warmth."

She chanced a look at him and wanted to throw something at him over the grin he tossed her. "No, I am fine. Go on to bed."

Too exasperated to care, Calvin moved across the room before she could get to her feet. He gathered her in his arms and smiled over the protest his hold forbid. "Humor me."

"I am not marrying you, Calvin Masterson." Willa wanted to scream over the look he gave her.

"Yes, you will, Willa."

"Why? You don't know me, and you certainly don't love me."

He stared at her for a moment, realizing what the problem might be. "You don't know that, Willa."

Her mouth opened to argue and snapped shut. She felt like a stiff board as he set her on the inside of the bed by the wall. She didn't breathe as he moved in behind her, and his arm came around her, pulling her against him. Every exquisite muscle in his body imprinted against her own.

"Calm down, honey. Take a deep breath and relax."

"How can I do that, Calvin?"

"Why can't you?"

"I don't, haven't slept with a man, Calvin." There, she said it.

He smiled into her hair, "I know."

"Oh." She tried to stop her body from shaking. "I really should go sleep by the fire, Calvin."

"You have slept with me, Willa."

"But that was to help you, Calvin."

"True, but we have slept together, Willa."

"But...."

His finger came to rest over her lips. "Hush, honey. Deep breaths, relax."

She tried to breathe but failed and pushed out of his hold to take a breath. "You make me nervous, Calvin."

He smiled to himself, knowing she didn't know how to lie to him. He pulled her back against his body and deliberately moved his hand gently up and down her thigh, causing her gown to ride up, exposing her soft skin. He knew he was succeeding in distracting her thoughts by the increase in her breaths. He thought for a moment that he should feel ashamed of his actions against her but brushed the thought away over the pleasure just touching her brought to him.

"You should stop that, Calvin."

"I don't think I can, Willa."

His warm breath felt extremely dangerous against her ear. The heat moved through her with lightning precision.

He could feel her confusion and wasn't surprised by it. Love seemed to be the problem for her. He decided she probably believed in fairy tales. "Relax against me, Willa, and sleep with me."

If he only knew how much she wanted to do just that, but Willa knew how he thought, what he wanted. "I won't marry you, Calvin."

"Hmm, you will, sweet girl, you will."

It took longer than he expected for her to fall asleep. He smiled against her hair and breathed in her essence. She didn't think he loved her, but Calvin was honest enough with himself to know he never felt like he did for her for anyone else, not even Ruth.

No, Willa was different, and he wanted her in his life. She was all soft and gentle. The wonder in her drew on his fascination with her, but what he felt went a lot deeper. He needed to find a way to show her how he felt. His arms increased their hold around her. Holding her to him filled Calvin with feelings he never experienced before.

His warm breath returned against her ear, and Willa couldn't help but smile. He made her feel whole. His touch warmed her in unknown ways. She knew she couldn't deny him anything, and he would be in his glory to know that truth. Marry him? Willa never thought love would come as it has with Calvin. She always thought she would meet someone someday, but she could never imagine like this, and here.

Willa took a deep breath and knew she would never be going back home. It was a feeling she couldn't shake.

Her hand unconsciously went about his own and held on. If she needed to end up with anyone she was glad it was Calvin.

CHAPTER FIVE

Willa stirred the grits she made and smiled. She figured he wouldn't sleep much longer smelling breakfast. The fact she managed to get out of bed without waking him made her want to laugh. He still held the pillow she moved into his arms.

Willa was glad about sleeping with him last night. But she felt like she didn't get much sleep. She wondered if she would get used to being beside him. She felt like she could crawl back in bed and sleep the day away.

The fresh milk smelled so good mixed into the oatmeal. She saved the ham for dinner. There would be enough for him to eat with what she cooked. She even felt hungry this morning. Willa didn't think he would lie there much longer; she knew he was awake from the scowl on his face and the fact that he threw the pillow at the bottom of the bed.

Willa started carrying the dishes over to the table by the bed. He was better now, but she still wanted him to take it easy. She placed his dishes down.

"Better get your own over here as well, Willa."

Her back was to him, so he couldn't see her smile. She carried her plates and silverware to the table and pulled up the chair. "Eat while it is all hot, Calvin."

He wanted to reach over and pull her back into bed. He refused to acknowledge that she managed to get away from him. Seeing the milk pail and filled egg basket, he realized she even went out and took care of the animals. He looked over at the window. He needed to get that rope up.

"The wind is starting to blow again, Calvin. It was clear a little while ago." She could see his anger marring his handsome features.

"It will probably blow all day, Willa."

"I brought in more wood and some on the porch. We should be fine."

He refused to smile at her. She should not have gone out without him. They needed to speak about some rules.

She could tell that nothing she said would quell his anger with her. Willa wasn't sure if it was because of getting out of bed or going outside. Either way, she figured she would hear about it.

Willa smiled over all the food he was eating. He must be feeling better this morning. She was glad she cooked as much as she did. She had a loaf of bread rising. The cornbread she made was nearly gone; she needed to grind down some more corn. "I need to remember to get some corn ears the next time I go to the barn."

"I'll bring some in. I don't want you to go out in the storm today, Willa."

Now that he finally said something, she bit her lips not to retaliate. "Alright, Calvin."

Willa didn't think he would listen to anything she might say.

His brow rose. She could tell he was angry. It surprised him.

"You are a very good cook, Willa."

"Thank you. I enjoy doing it."

"Like the animals."

She smiled, "Yes, them as well."

"In the spring, we will get a hog."

"I am afraid you will need to teach me how to cure it. I've not done that before."

"I have a smokehouse on the other side of the barn that I use for the meat."

"The ham has a very good flavor, Calvin."

"I learned from my father how to do it all."

"He must have been a very smart man, Calvin. And you have taken after him."

Willa realized she said too much and rose to leave the table. Picking up her breakfast plate, Calvin's hand covered hers and stopped her.

"You hardly ate, Willa."

"I am full."

"I doubt it."

She didn't try to pull her hand away; his grip was too tight. "Calvin?"

"Please, stay with me a while longer, Willa. We need to discuss some things."

She slowly retook her seat. Willa wondered what could be wrong.

"I wanted to speak to you about going outside. I ask you to let me know when you do so. It can be dangerous."

She wasn't sure what to say.

Calvin swore her eyes grew twice as large as normal over his announcement. He saw her fingers begin to shake. "Willa, there are wild animals about, especially in the winter."

"Animals?"

"Yes, like bears, cougars, and boars. They can be very aggressive if they are hungry. Which makes them very dangerous."

"Oh, should I carry a gun?"

She looked so scared he wished he hadn't said anything. "This is why you need to let me know when you are going out, say to the barn or getting wood. I can check and be sure it is safe, Willa."

"Alright, I can do that. Maybe you should teach me how to shoot." She looked at the long gun over the fireplace.

Calvin almost laughed, but he knew she was serious. "No, you should be fine. I am here."

"What if you are gone?"

"Let me think about it, Willa."

"Yes, you probably should. I never realized a danger existed." Willa stood and started clearing the table to cover her nervousness. "Bears? Dang."

Calvin immediately rose and followed her. He waited for her to put down the dishes she held and then pulled her into his arms. "It will be fine, Willa. We just need to be careful."

She buried her face against his chest, and he could feel her tears. "I am sorry, Calvin. I have never dealt with this sort of danger before. I mean, I took self-defense classes, but I don't think I could tackle a bear or lion. I don't even know what a boar is."

She looked up at him with the saddest face. Calvin groaned, and his hand cupped her head and pulled her back against him. "I'm so sorry, Willa. I want to keep you safe."

Willa sobbed against his chest. She couldn't stop herself.

Calvin hugged her closer. His large hand spanned her back to help calm her. Seeing how much his warning affected her, he was glad he brought it up. "One thing you don't want to do is run. If you run, they will chase you."

She nodded against his chest, and then he felt her go limp. Calvin cradled her in his arms and moved to the chair with her. He held her, realizing she fainted. His lips brushed her brow. Calvin looked at her and took a deep breath. She really had no idea about this world. Like the milk and eggs, it was all new and unknown to her. He silently groaned over the truth of it. His fingers brushed back the bangs that fell across her brow. "You will marry me, Willa. You will only be safe with me."

CHAPTER SIX

Willa snuggled deeper into the arms, holding her. "Calvin?"

His hold around her tightened. "I'm here, Willa."

She tried to push off of him but failed over his hold on her. "Hush, take it slow."

"What happened, Calvin?"

"You fainted."

She pushed against him again and, this time sat up. For a second, she felt dizzy and let her head go back against his chest. "I don't faint, Calvin."

He smiled, his fingers went through her hair, and he kissed the top of her head. "No, of course you don't."

Willa tried to remember what might have happened. "Bears?"

"And lions."

"I remember, now."

Calvin didn't say anything. He just held her. "It is something you need to know about. Oh, add wolves to the list."

She bit her lip and moved deeper into his hold. "I know."

"So, we won't be scared, just cautious."

"That sounds good, Calvin."

His hand cupped her head. He admitted to himself that it was an act to keep her in his arms more than anything else. He wanted to hold her all the time. Feeling her against him felt right. He kept holding her and rocked the chair slowly as she relaxed. He placed his cheek against her head. He closed his eyes and breathed in that part of Willa that already became a part of him.

He realized he needed to be careful and not smother her. But keeping her safe suddenly became extremely important to him. He wanted to groan over the truth of it. She was so fragile, yet in some ways strong. His head went back hard against the chair. He couldn't get the image of her holding their child out of his head. Hell, they hadn't even made love.

• • ༄ • •

Willa wanted to stretch, and yet she held back. She slowly opened her eyes. Willa looked around, knowing she was in bed, and Calvin lay beside her. She couldn't remember going to bed. His arm lay across her stomach in a protective hold. The only way to dislodge him would be to wake him. Admitting he made her feel safe bothered her a bit. She realized he stepped all over her independence. She thought about the animals. Hearing the wind, she knew she wouldn't go out, especially after they talked. Willa turned a bit and snuggled in closer to him. His hold tightened against her movement.

"You are awake, Willa."

"Yes, Calvin, I am."

"I took care of the animals, Willa."

"Oh, good, I was wondering."

"They will be fine until tomorrow. I also cut some ham up for sandwiches."

"Alright, Calvin."

"We still have some things to discuss, Willa."

"Oh, I don't know, Calvin. Wild animals are about all I can take in right now."

He smiled against her head and silently kissed her. "Yes, I know it is a lot, Willa."

"I still think you should teach me how to shoot."

He took a deep breath, "I agree. Once the snow slows down, I will start the lessons. You were right. I may not be here at times, so you need to know how to defend yourself."

She tried to keep breathing evenly. "Good, I will listen."

He wanted to laugh over her concession. "It helps to learn if you do."

She couldn't hold back any longer and giggled against his chest. When he moved closer, she waved him off. "Sorry, it all sounds so civilized. I get nervous, and I have to laugh; so sorry, Calvin."

He huffed against her head. "It is okay to do, Willa. Glad you told me."

"What else do we need to discuss, Calvin?"

He moved over her. Willa's hands came to rest against his chest as he loomed over her. His strong thighs locked her beneath him. "You need to listen to me, Willa."

She looked up into his serious glare upon her. "I will, Calvin."

"Good, because this is even more important than the animal dangers."

She nodded and bit her lip. "Bigger?"

"Yes, Willa. Much bigger and just as important."

"Okay, Calvin. I am listening."

He rose above her, straddling her hips. "Remember when I said you would be my wife, Willa?"

She nodded and said, "Yes, Calvin."

"I want you to know I meant every word, Willa."

"I heard you, Calvin. Though,..." His finger covered her lips and stopped her words. "I know what you will say, Willa, but it doesn't matter. Not here, it doesn't matter." He smiled at her over the questioning in her gaze upon him. "You see, when you came here, what was your life stayed behind. I do believe that, Willa. Your life is here, with me, now, Willa. You said I couldn't love you, but Willa, I do love you, and I want to keep you safe and loved in my arms, only mine, Willa."

She took a deep breath and wanted to say something, but he stopped her. His head shook, "all your arguments won't change what has happened to you, now to both of us."

He moved his finger away to let her talk. She wet her lips but couldn't find anything to say to stop what he started, so she snapped her mouth shut over the smile he gave her.

"I have every intention of becoming your husband, Willa. I promise to love you, hold you, answer your questions, and keep you safe. I will be here for you in sickness and health, just as I know you will be for me. I, Calvin Paul Masterson, take you, Willamena Garrison, as my lawful wedded wife to love and to hold until death do us part." Calvin took hold of her hand and slipped a ring on her finger. "This was my mother's ring, Willa. It has nothing to do with Ruth."

She couldn't help but smile over his truthful statement. "I don't have a ring for you, Calvin."

He nodded, "You don't need one, Willa. Your heart holds me to you. It is stronger than a ring, Willa."

Willa thought for a moment that she should protest his hold on her but dismissed the thought. Her hand reached up and cupped his cheek. "I, Willamena Garrison, take you, Calvin Paul Masterson, as my lawful and beloved husband. To love and to hold, in sickness and in health, until death do us part."

Calvin's head turned, and his lips kissed her palm. "We are married now, Willa."

"Wow."

It was his turn to laugh, and he did against her breasts. Her hand came and held his head there, and she wondered if she could keep him there forever.

CHAPTER SEVEN

Calvin's fingers ran through the soft lengths of Willa's hair. His other arm held her against his chest, where she lay after their night of lovemaking. As he instinctively knew she was certainly a virgin and new to the whole experience of making love. "But a fast learner, my sweet lover."

He smiled, remembering how she learned and then wanted to try more. They wouldn't grow tired of each other. He tried not to think of Ruth and how she detested lovemaking. Even when she became pregnant, she hated the child; she didn't want it right from the first. Calvin often wondered if she died because she didn't want the child. He couldn't imagine Willa feeling like that. They were so different, and he thanked God for her.

His lips brushed her hair; she told him she couldn't believe she had married him. He told her it was because they loved each other. She looked at him for a while and then smiled and said she did love him. His wonder hadn't ceased since she told him that.

She snuggled back against him, and he grinned. For a lady so dead set against marrying him she sure showed him how glad she was that they did get married. Though, she reminded him that it was his insistence that made it happen.

"I think we should stay right here all day, Calvin." She couldn't stop the pleased moan that came from her as he nuzzled her neck and played with her ear. He knew how crazy it made her.

"I would love to, Willa. But I do need to check the traps. The furs give us money for things like the pig."

She sighed against his chest. "Yes, I know. You should take me with you and teach me how to set the traps."

"How about I bring back some meat for a stew or roast."

"I guess that will do." She giggled against him and set him on fire.

"Oh, lady, what you do to me is probably outlawed."

37

"Then they will need to put us in the same cell." The heat of their kiss raced through both of them. Willa pulled him over her and smiled.

.. ⌘ ..

Willa finished milking the cow and smiled. "It is a marvelous place."

She thought about Calvin. He was out checking his traplines, and she felt he would have a good catch. Spring brought the animals out. He would have a lot of furs for trading when they went into town. Odd, the way she'd been feeling, she thought maybe she should stay here and let him go alone into town.

Willa smiled to herself. Her hand covered the lower part of her stomach. "Am I?" She twirled in place and hoped it was so. "Boy or girl, we will love either of you."

"Yes, we will."

She stopped fast over hearing Calvin's deep voice. "Hi, you are home early."

"You look happy, Willa."

She laughed up to the barn rafters and kept moving in a circle with her arms out. "I am, Calvin. Happier than I ever imagined I could be."

He slowly walked towards her, silently thanking God for bringing this marvelous lady to him. "And what are we so happy about, my love?"

He gathered her in his arms and pulled her to him. Her lips were sweet and wanting, and Calvin drank them in.

When he finally pulled back, she smiled at him. "Well, Mr. Masterson, I have a feeling I might be pregnant, and that, my dear, sweet man, is something to be very happy about. Of course, I know absolutely nothing about having a baby, so I will need a lot of help with this one, Calvin."

He swung her around in the circle and laughed. "I've had a feeling you might be."

"Really? My goodness, I sure hope we are right. Won't it be beautiful, a child, our child, something we created."

"Created in love, Willa. That is what makes it so special."

Her hands were on his shoulders, "Yes, our child will be very special, Calvin."

She leaned down and took his lips in with her own as he lowered her against his virile body.

Her hands framed his face as she gloried in the man in her life. "Maybe I could have two, twins."

He laughed, "One will be enough."

"Yes, you are right. One will do. There will be others."

"You are so sure, Willa."

"I am, you see, when you love someone like I do you, well, Calvin, it is all part of the marvelous experience." Her lips brushed his. "And you, my dear husband, will always be a grand experience in my book."

They kissed for a long time in the shadows of the barn. In wonderful slowness, Calvin lowered Willa to the ground. Her toes sunk into the damp earth. "The ground is thawing, Calvin."

His head went back in laughter as he looked at her feet. "You do like to go barefoot, Willa."

"Oh, my yes, Calvin. It is wonderful to feel the earth. Everything is turning green and beautiful. I can even smell the blooms that are now happening. How did the trapline do?"

"Very well, Willa. I have some meat to smoke and a nice rabbit for you to cook."

"Sounds good. I have a bunch of cornbread ready."

"I do love your cornbread, Willa."

"And a nice rabbit will taste wonderful with it."

"With this batch of furs, I will have enough to get that pig to put up for winter."

"That is wonderful, Calvin."

He rubbed his nose against hers. "And yes, I will look for a couple of lambs for the wool you want."

"Oh yes, the fiber would be great to have on hand. I will need to make a blanket for the baby."

"How does the crochet hook work?"

"Very well, and I've even conquered the stitches I need to use. It is amazing that I remembered them at all. My grandmother would be pleased to know I paid attention to her."

"Have you decided how many rows you need for the vegetable garden?"

"Yes, and I wrote it down for you."

His hand covered her lower stomach. "Good, I don't want you to hoe the garden, Willa."

"I can plant, though?"

"Yes, you can plant. Just make sure you wear your gun. Winter may be over, but the predators are still around."

"I have it on as you instructed."

"Good." He smiled at her. "I will be out to plow up the field for the corn, then the hay."

"That will be amazing to see, Calvin. If I can help, let me know."

"You can finish de-earing the corn. Then that will be ready for the planting."

"What about the oats?"

"I have a bag ready for planting. I'll need to get another for next year."

"You best get a cat. It will help stop the mice from eating the stores."

"A cat?"

"Yes, that furry thing that catches smaller, not so furry things. I remember my aunt Nellie having them at her farm. Of course, now I know that they mated with the bobcats in the area, and that is why the kittens were so darn wild. Boy, I used to get all scratched up from those kittens?"

His head went down to her shoulder as he laughed. Laughter was something that Willa brought back into his life, and he loved her for it.

CHAPTER EIGHT

Willa heard the hoofbeats in the yard and stopped what she was doing to leave the barn. What she saw stopped her and started a slow, dangerous fire burning inside her. "The audacity of that woman."

She walked over to the wood stump and grabbed the ax. Willa took a deep breath and swung the ax into the thick stump, knowing she shouldn't keep holding it. "No, I might use it."

Calvin swore the ax went well over an inch into the thick wood, and he knew Willa was more than just angry. Not that he could blame her. He kept Mildred away from him, but not before the woman kissed him, and Willa didn't miss a second of it. She came forward in pure attack mode, and he couldn't do anything but keep Mildred at arm's length away from him. The woman was trying to grab him again to kiss him.

Willa reached out and grabbed hold of the woman's hair and pulled her from Calvin, tossing her to the ground. "Okay, you skank whore get your filthy hands off of my husband."

"Who are you?"

Willa stood over the bitch on the ground and wanted to kick her. "I am Calvin's wife. I suggest you get your whoring ass back on that horse and solicit some other poor man. Now! Before I shoot you, for throwing yourself at him!"

"You can't be his wife." She sounded so smug that Willa felt like puking. When the woman shoved herself to her feet and started coming at Willa, she brought her fist back and clobbered the filthy bitch in the face.

Willa felt Calvin's arm come around her and move her behind him. "Mildred, she is my wife, in God's eyes, and what you did was wrong. I am surprised at you."

"She isn't your wife! You were supposed to marry me!"

"I never even courted you, Mildred. Wherever did you get an idea like that?"

The woman's mouth dropped open over Calvin's words. Willa wanted to smack her again and would have if Calvin wasn't holding her. "Get back on your horse, you whore!"

Calvin held Willa against his side to keep her from going after Mildred again. "I think you better do it, Mildred. Don't bother coming back here again."

"I will shoot her, Calvin."

He wanted to smile but held it back. "I know you will, Willa."

When the woman started to advance on her again, Willa called out to Calvin to look out! "The bitch has a gun in her hand!"

Willa broke Calvin's hold and raced forward, raised up, and kicked the damn gun out of the woman's hold. Then she clobbered her again and put her to the ground, but not before picking up the gun. "Get the hell out of here! You are insane."

Calvin's arms encircled her again, and Willa leaned back against him. "She is one crazy bitch, Calvin."

"She is also the preacher's daughter."

Willa huffed over that announcement, "We won't be going to that church. I don't care if it is the only one in town. My child won't be baptized there, either."

Calvin's hand went over the swell of their child in a protective measure. They both stood and watched the woman get on her horse. "Don't come back, ever, Mildred. And I will tell your father what you did today."

The woman jerked the animal around and whipped it into a gallop out of the yard.

"What kind of a nut is that, Calvin?"

"I don't know, Willa. She certainly never acted like that before.

Are you okay, Willa?"

"I am angrier than I think I have ever been in my life. Did I forget to mention how jealous I must be?"

Calvin shook his head, smiled into her hair, and kissed her neck, "Nope, but I sure know now."

"Me too."

. . ⌘ . .

That night, Calvin held Willa close to him and sighed. He smiled over her reminder that she did take self-defense classes. He wasn't sure when she first told him what it was, but he saw it in action today against Mildred. He thought the woman was fortunate to be alive.

They did speak about the baptism of their child, and Willa informed him that the bible would take care of it and the bible would baptize their child. She also said that God surrounded them in his glory right here in this land. Nothing could ruin it, not even a deranged woman.

Calvin closed his eyes and thanked the Lord for sending Willa to him.

CHAPTER NINE

Willa passed Calvin the bag of sandwiches. "Are you sure you have everything?"

He leaned down from the buckboard and kissed her. "Yes, I am sure. You have your gun?"

She patted the gun on her hip in the holster he made for her. "Right here, Calvin."

"Make sure you wear it, Willa."

"I will, promise."

"I should be back in two days, Willa."

"Okay, I will keep an eye out for you." She smiled at him, not liking the worried look on his face. "You stay safe, Calvin."

"I best get going."

"Yes. I will keep the door locked, too."

He smiled, and it took all his willpower to get the horse and wagon moving. Leaving her wasn't easy. Looking back and seeing how much the baby showed on her tiny frame made the whole leave even more difficult. "Damn, she should come with me."

If only she hadn't been so sick the last few days. Willa called it morning sickness. He didn't argue with her even though she got sick at all times of the day and night. The baby was taking a lot out of her, but she'd not hear any of it. The sun rose and shined on the child. He shook his head and huffed over the truth of it. They both wanted this child so much. He didn't like leaving her. Calvin prayed Willa would be fine in his absence.

He thought of all the supplies they needed and knew he must go into town. Calvin also knew he needed to speak to the reverend about Mildred. He swore he saw her up in the ridge the other day. He told himself he must be imagining it.

· · ❧ · ·

Willa watched until the wagon faded from sight. She turned to go inside and start the bread she wanted to make. Once inside she did turn and lock the door as she promised Calvin she would. Willa thought it was foolish, but she did promise.

She wouldn't go outside again until this evening to care for the animals. Willa hoped Calvin could find some lambs. She was nearly out of the yarn that was in Ruth's chest. "At least it is getting used." Right now, she wished she had taken a course in working and dying the fleece. "I could use that skill." Calvin did make her a spinning wheel to turn the fleece into yarn.

Trial and error became Willa's motto of late. There was so much to learn. She smiled deciding she did pretty good at her attempts to do things. "Like making butter and canning berries for jam. A lot of it is just common sense." She smiled over the row of blackberry jam she made. If nothing else, they would have syrup for pancakes. She giggled, knowing that was probably what would happen.

Her brow creased in worry over how Calvin would do with the minister. He put a lot of store in that man. Having to tell him what his daughter did wouldn't go over well with Calvin. Willa decided the woman must have lost it mentally to do what she did.

The day slipped by for Willa. The bread came out good, and that made her smile. She looked outside and knew she needed to go feed the animals. Willa threw the shawl around her and knotted it in the front. The evenings were still chilly, and she needed to milk the cow.

She sucked in the brisk air as she walked to the barn. The apple tree in the yard was filled with blooms, and she smiled, "they will be nice to have."

Before she reached the barndoor, a sudden flash and then a burning sensation struck her. The force was so great that it spun Willa about before she hit the ground. For a moment, she lay there trying to figure out what had happened. She felt the warmth flooding her shoulder and reached up to discover what it might be.

"It is wet." She pulled her hand back and stared at the blood that filled her palm. "Oh dear."

Willa knew she'd been shot, and she pulled the gun from her side into her hand. She could hear footsteps coming her way. She took a deep breath and forced herself to roll to her side. "You!"

"He isn't here to save you. I will have him when you die."

Willa saw the woman begin to lift her arm and knew she was going to shoot her again. Willa didn't hesitate and fired the gun. She watched in horrid fascination as Mildred fell back over the impact and didn't get up after falling to the ground.

For a minute, Willa just lay there and wondered what happened. She blinked and looked around. "The sun is setting." Some inner strength told Willa she needed to move. Laying there bleeding would only bring the predators out. Willa took her shawl and folded it the best she could before putting it against the wound. She remembered reading once that you needed to stop the blood flow, especially from a bullet. The distance to the house was further than the barn. Willa picked the barn.

She started pulling herself to the small door on her good side. The side she was shot on, she couldn't seem to move her arm, and it hurt too much to try any longer. It took a long time to reach the door, but she managed to get it open and crawl through it. With her fingers, she pulled the door shut. "I made it into the barn, much safer than outside."

Willa didn't know how long she lay there, deciding she probably passed out. She couldn't see much when she came to. It was too dark.

· · ⚬ · ·

"What do you mean she isn't here?"

"She's been gone over a week now, Calvin."

"You do know that your daughter is crazy. She tried to kill my wife! Claiming we were supposed to be married."

"I'm sorry, Calvin. I don't know what happened to Mildred."

"I need to get home."

"Do you really think she would kill someone?"

Calvin looked at the man, "Yes, I know she will."

Without another word, Calvin pushed the man out of his way and headed out the door. He hadn't even unpacked the wagon. He boarded and turned the wagon around to head back to the house. An awful feeling settled in his gut and nothing he did would dimmish the force of it.

"Dear Willa, stay safe, my love."

CHAPTER TEN

The mooing cow finally penetrated Willa's thoughts. "Oh, sweet girl, I'm sorry. I don't have it in me to get to you."

No, she knew she couldn't move. It seemed all her energy deserted her.

Her hand went over the baby, and she wanted to cry. "You hang in there, little one, just don't give up. Your daddy will come...he has to."

She realized it was daylight out, but Willa knew she wouldn't reach the house. There was a large puddle of blood beside her, and she groaned over the fact. She took a deep breath but couldn't move. "We will just wait here for Daddy." Willa could feel the darkness moving in on her, and she couldn't do anything to stop it.

• • ⁕ • •

Calvin wanted to scream. He could hear the horse beats behind him, knowing the reverend was following him. He prayed he would reach her in time. Calvin knew without a doubt that Willa was hurt and in danger. He could feel it.

They reached the yard, and it was all he could do to pull the wagon to a stop before jumping down. He raced to the house but saw Mildred and stopped. She laid there dead with the gun still in her hand.

Calvin called out to Willa and groaned over the lack of an answer. He called out again and started walking until he saw the blood. Calvin dropped to his knees, knowing it was too much blood. "Too much."

The reverend was standing beside him. "Oh, Calvin."

Calvin saw the blood trail and started following it to the barn. He started running, knowing it was where she was headed. "Come on, Willa, where are you?"

He pulled the door open and raced inside. He didn't need to go very far when he saw her lying on the ground. "Oh, Willa."

Calvin went to his knees beside her and gently pulled her over and out of the pool of blood. His head went to her chest, and he didn't breathe until he heard her faint heartbeat. As cautious as he could be, he gathered her into his arms and stood up.

"Is she alive, Calvin?"

"Just barely. She's lost an awful lot of blood."

"Is she pregnant?"

"Yes, about six months."

"Oh, dear God."

Calvin ignored the man and started walking to the house. He kicked the door open and took her to the bed. Calvin carefully laid Willa out on the bed. From the blood on his hand, he knew the bullet had gone through her shoulder. He ripped the dress so he could tend to the wound, then realized the man was still there. "Get out, get out now, or so help me, I will put you out there with your insane daughter."

The man backed up with his hands raised. "Calvin..."

"Get out!"

Calvin moved about the house to get the items he needed. Stitching the wound was the first thing on his list. It was the only way to stop her from losing more blood. He didn't even want to think about the child, knowing she might lose it.

"I told him..."

He stopped over hearing her speak. He knelt and took hold of her hand. "What, my love, who did you tell?"

Willa tried to smile, but she could barely open her eyes. "I told him that his daddy would come."

Calvin kissed her fingers in his clasp and fought back his sobs. "I'm going to fix you up, Willa."

"He is strong, Calvin. He will make it."

With that said, she passed out.

Calvin placed her hand on her stomach and wiped his eyes. "I sure hope you are right, Willa."

He went to work and hoped he could save them both.

. . ✿ . .

It was dark when Calvin finally took a break and walked outside. He was surprised to see the reverend still there, sitting on the steps.

"How is she, Calvin?"

"She is sleeping now. I stitched the wounds and got the bleeding stopped."

"The baby?"

"For now, he is still alive."

"A boy?"

"Willa said it was a boy and that he was strong. I figure she is right."

"It is hard to imagine that Mildred caused all this."

"Something went wrong with her mind."

"We will need to pray about it in church."

Calvin took a deep breath. "We won't be coming to church anymore. Willa and I have discussed it and made the decision."

"But Calvin..."

"No buts, if she lives through this and our child makes it, we will thank God, and we will praise him, but not in the church, and that is the end of it. As Willa says, God is all around us, right here."

"She is right, he is. I am very sorry this happened."

"You best take your daughter and leave. I need to tend to my wife and child."

With that, Calvin walked back into the house and locked the door behind him.

He went to the kitchen, mashed some of the bread and an egg in milk, and put it on to warm. Willa needed nourishment to regain some of her strength. He hoped she would be able to take some and keep it down.

Calvin walked over to the bed with the bowl. He needed to hold her up a bit so she could swallow. He gathered her in his arms and started talking to her. "You need to eat something, Willa, for the baby and get stronger. You lost a lot of blood, my love. Come on, let's see if you can get some of this down."

Calvin pressed the spoon to her lips, and he saw her try to take it in. He waited to make sure she could swallow it before trying another spoonful. He kept feeding her for some time before he knew she had fallen asleep again. He looked and realized she took in nearly half the bowl and smiled. He hoped it meant she would recover. His hand covered their child, and Calvin sucked in his breath, feeling the child move beneath his hand. "You will make it, son. She said you would." He swore the baby moved over his words as the tears rolled down his cheeks. "I never should have left you, Willa."

Her hand squeezed his. She wished she had more strength to talk with him. Her eyes were barely open, but she could see his tears. She put all her energy into reaching up and wiping them away. "We will make it, Calvin."

"He moved, Willa."

She managed to smile, "Saying hi to his father."

Calvin kissed her palm. "I love you, Willa."

"And I love you, Calvin."

"Get some sleep, Willa, and heal."

Willa tossed her head, knowing she needed to tell him. "I had to shoot her, Calvin. She was going to shoot me again."

"It is over, sweet girl. You did right."

Calvin pulled her up and held her. Her fingers took hold of his shirt, and her head snuggled up against him. He noticed before that Willa didn't or couldn't use her injured arm or hand. He hoped it would heal. Calvin smiled, she would make it, and they would deal with it, as she liked to say.

CHAPTER ELEVEN

Calvin came in with the milk and eggs to find Willa thrashing about on the bed. She'd been having nightmares over the shooting. He hoped that was all it was. He did fear she would get a fever. He set everything down and moved over to her, taking hold of her to keep her from moving about. He checked, the stitches were still in and no bleeding. "Come on, sweet girl, settle down; it is just a dream."

"She is insane, Calvin. She keeps telling me when I die, she will marry you."

"Well, that is all in her head. I won't ever marry her or anyone. I am married to you, Willa. I love you. Now, try to get some sleep. Our baby needs you to sleep and grow stronger."

She started to calm down in his arms. He knew she felt safe in his hold. He hoped she would get some sleep this time. Calvin eased her back into the bed and pulled the covers around her. He went over and added a log to the fire. His brow creased and not just in worry over Willa. He hadn't got the oat field planted, "at least the corn is planted." He looked at it this morning and was pleased with the shoots coming up. He needed to get the vegetables planted in Willa's Garden as well.

"There is so much to do." Yet, he worried about leaving her for any length of time. Today, he would try to get her garden planted. He managed to get the rows ready yesterday. "If nothing else, we will have them. We do need to get the hay planted; the animals can't exist on the corn alone.

When you are better we will go to town for the supplies. You will like that, Willa."

"I will like that, Calvin."

He looked down at her and smiled. "How do you feel?"

"Stronger, I think I am actually hungry."

He huffed, "now that is a good sign."

She took hold of his hand and placed it over the baby. "He is moving, and he hears you, Calvin. We need a good, strong name for him."

"My dad's name was Jacob."

"Oh, I like that name very much. Jacob is good, Calvin."

"Let me put some milk on to warm."

"You might want to add some of that blackberry syrup to it. That will taste good."

Calvin huffed. They both laughed over her attempt at jam, but they did have a good supply of syrup.

"You know, Calvin. I think I am strong enough for you to do the planting."

"You heard me."

She smiled, "Yes, and it is important that you get it done."

"But..."

"No buts, Calvin. I will be fine here. Heck, we can even set up a line of chairs and things for me to hold onto if I need to walk. Take a step and sit. Besides, I need to move a bit. I'm stiff." She saw him look at her arm. "Yeah, I think the bullet killed the nerves in my arm. I don't think it will ever come back like it was, but at least it was my left side and not the right."

Calvin chewed his cheek to keep his temper down over the fact.

"I do think I will have enough strength in it to hold our son while I feed him. So, that is a good thing, Calvin." Willa wanted to defuse his anger.

She knew him well. "Yes, it is a good thing. He is getting so big, Willa."

Her hand moved over his, "he is growing and getting ready to come to us. I can hardly wait to hold him, Calvin."

"At least you stopped getting sick all the time."

"And I am getting stronger. Maybe we can go into town before he comes."

Calvin smiled at her to stop her worry, he knew her too. "Yes, I think we probably can. Let's give it a couple more weeks , and then plan the trip."

"That sounds good, Calvin."

"But right now, I am going out to plant your garden. That is almost as important as the hay. We will use all the vegetables."

"How is the apple tree doing?"

"It is getting baby apples on it." Calvin thought for a moment. "Why don't you come out with me? You can sit on the steps and lean into them. That way, you can see the baby apples and direct me on the planting."

"Oh yes, I would love to go out. I can sort the seeds for you while I sit there."

He walked to her and smiled, "Yes, you can. Come on, let's go plant."

Calvin had a feeling if this worked that he could put her on the wagon and take her out to the field with him. He did think she would wear out fast, but she would enjoy being outside for a while.

Willa was very excited as he lowered her onto the step. "Now, Willa, you have the post right here to lean against and hang onto."

"Okay, Calvin. Where are the seeds and which do you want first?"

"Let's get the leaf vegetables in first, then the roots."

"Okay, let's start with the spinach and kale. Those two are strong. I will get the celery and onions ready for the next batch."

"That sounds good, Willa." Calvin took the handful of seeds she gave him for the spinach and told her to hold onto the kale. It didn't take him long to get the spinach row completed. He went back and got the kale seeds from her. "It will be nice to have greens, Willa."

"Oh, I know, a nice rabbit stew with fresh greens, yummy."

"You really are hungry."

It was good to hear her laughing. Calvin soon had the celery and onions in and started on the potatoes. Willa cut the potatoes for planting as he put in the first batch.

"The apple tree is full of new growth, we should get a nice crop, Calvin."

"Yes, and they keep for winter."

"Are you ready for the squash?"

"Yes, all around the outside, and I saved a spot for the watermelon at the far end." When she didn't answer him, he spun about. "You lasted longer than I thought you would, my dear wife."

He took the seeds out of her hands and set them on the other side of the step so that he could gather her up. She leaned into him, and he barely caught her soft words.

"It is so beautiful, Calvin."

Calvin put his cheek against her head, "Yes, it is very beautiful." His lips brushed her hair as they walked over to the bed. "Get some sleep, pretty lady. I will check and see if we have a rabbit for dinner."

He made sure her bad arm was on the outside as she snuggled into the covers. Calvin may hide it well, but he was very angry over the damage she suffered. He did hope she might get some use back into her hand. They would have to start exercising, as she mentioned, and he hoped it would help. "Knots coming up."

Calvin had the board ready for the variety of knots to go on it. Willa told him that knots would make her use her fingers and hand. They knew it was a long shot to work, but Calvin would help her all he could. He also decided to make the board moveable. That way, she could have it in the house or on the porch.

. . ⚮ . .

It was the second day Calvin went out to plant the hay field. Willa reached and grabbed the post to help her sit on the step. She scooted off the top step and landed on the next one. She looked at her pole leaning against the banister at the bottom of the steps. Willa was determined to take care of the animals so he wouldn't have to do it. "Too many chores for one person."

She reached the next to the last step at the bottom and pulled herself to her feet. She reached over and grabbed her stick to help her walk. She wasn't as weak as she had been but still tired too soon for her liking. Willa headed to the barn.

When she entered the darkened area, all the heads swung around to see her, and the chickens came running. "It is my first time out here since that day. Hi all, let's hope I can do this." She walked over and picked up the egg basket, she figured it was the easiest one to tackle first. Willa gathered over a dozen eggs and smiled. "An omelet works too."

She placed the basket over by the door and headed back to gather the stool and pail for the cow. "Now, lady, I may need to experiment to find the best way to do this, so be patient."

Willa got the stool in place and sat down, laying her pole beside her. She moved the pail under the cow to where she thought the milk would flow and leaned into the cow's stomach. "Okay, pretty girl, let's get this going."

Using only her good hand wasn't as fast as using two, but the milk hit the bucket and kept coming.

Calvin pulled up the wagon and heard Willa's song coming from the barn. He looked, and her pole was gone. His steps quickened to reach the barn and see what she was up to. He immediately saw the full egg basket and the food in the bins. The chickens were also pecking away at the corn she threw down for them. He moved further in and saw her milking the cow. Her eyes were closed, and if she weren't singing, he would swear she was sleeping. The milk pail was nearly full. "I think you got it, Willa."

"Hi, Calvin. I was going to leave the pail out here for you to carry in, but you are here, so that is good."

"How are you feeling, Willa?"

"Tired, but then I knew I would be." She picked up her pole and put the stool away. "I should be able to carry the egg basket."

"Alright, Willa. I have the milk." Calvin watched as she picked up the basket and placed it over her bad arm in the sling she must have made.

"Yes, it will work, Calvin."

"Looks good, Willa."

"So, do we have a rabbit?"

"Yes, we do, and what a great dinner it will be."

"The garden looks great, Calvin. Everything is growing. I even saw carrot tops peaking up, I bet potatoes are also coming in."

"I take it, I should check for the roast you want to make." Calvin huffed, he leaned over and kissed her.

She smiled at him. "That would be a good thing to do, Calvin."

"Would celery and onions be on that list as well?"

"If they are ready, I still have an onion."

"Good."

"I will start dinner."

He wanted to tell her she'd done enough, but he could see she wouldn't listen. Willa was determined to be better. "The rabbit is in the roaster."

"Oh good, thank you."

Calvin walked with her to the kitchen, putting up the eggs and milk. He watched her for a moment as she scooted around the counter. "I'll go to the garden, Willa."

"Good, I'll start on the roast."

He watched from the door for a minute as she fed the stove wood to build up the fire. He smiled to himself. She was certainly determined. He did pull some carrots and a couple of potatoes. Calvin also cut a few stalks off one of the celery plants. Calvin washed everything and put them in the pan to bring to her.

"Here you go, Willa. You have a nice variety for the roast."

"Oh, my, that looks great, Calvin."

"You want me to cut them up for you?"

"If you don't mind." She wanted to say no, but then she did feel tired and didn't want him to worry. "How did the planting go today?"

"I finished the hay field today. And the corn is nearly knee-high now."

"My goodness, it is growing very fast. It must be all the snow we got this winter."

"I think so, which means the hay should do well."

"Then I think we need to plan our trip into town, Calvin. I figure I have about a month before the baby comes. What do you think?"

"A month sounds about right. Are you up to the trip?"

"Well, like you said you can put a post up for me hold onto by the seat."

"Yes, I have that ready to be put on the wagon. You can also put a quilt in the back if you need to lie down."

"That sounds good, I do still get tired easy. I did good today, Calvin. I want to try to take over the animals again, so you don't have to do it. The only thing is you will need to carry in the milk pail, until I get a little stronger."

"That isn't a problem, Willa."

"Good. If I have a problem, I will tell you, Calvin. I wasn't sure I could milk with one hand, but I did alright. I did get tired, but not bad, and each day, I will get stronger."

He pulled her into his arms. "Yes, you will. I am going to put up the knot board tonight."

She leaned back and looked up at him. "That will be good. I need to do it."

"I put a hook on it so it can be moved to the porch. That way, you can sit outside when you want."

"Thank you, Calvin. I will like that. I do like to be outside. It is probably because of winter."

She giggled into his chest, and Calvin wanted to moan. He looked down and saw her bare feet and huffed.

Willa giggled harder and hugged him. "Soon, Calvin. I am getting stronger."

He nuzzled her neck and nipped her. "I can hardly wait, hardly being the main word."

CHAPTER TWELVE

"How are you doing, Willa?"

"I haven't fallen off the seat yet, so I'd say pretty good."

Calvin's brow furrowed over the grip she maintained on the post. "If you need a break, just say so."

"No, I am good, Calvin. Maybe coming home, I will need to lie down in the back."

"I will make sure you have a spot."

"Okay."

"Let's go over the list again." Calvin waited for her to pull out the list. She managed to hold the list with her bad hand, and he smiled over her accomplishment. She told him that between the milking and knots, she gained some feeling in her fingers.

They entered town, and Willa was surprised at how congested and large it looked. She also saw all the people staring at her. She couldn't stand it. "Calvin, why are they staring at me?"

"They are people from church. Just ignore them, Willa."

"Oh, okay, Calvin." She didn't understand, but she didn't want any trouble either. And she knew Calvin would not back down from a fight. She was going to take her arm out of the sling, but then decided she might need the support after the bumpy ride. She already felt tired but refused to say anything to Calvin. They had a lot to do. The first stop was the fur trading company. Calvin told her that is where they would get the money they needed for the supplies.

She already told him she would stay on the wagon and wait for him while he conducted business. But with all the people staring at her, she wondered if she should go with him.

Calvin reached over and gripped her arm. It was the bad one, but he knew she felt him. "Will you be alright, Willa?"

She looked at him, "I will be, they might not."

His brow rose, and he nodded. He smiled and kissed her brow. "You, my lovely wife, may do whatever you feel necessary."

"Thank you, I just might."

"I shouldn't be too long, Willa."

"You take all the time you need, Calvin. I am a big girl and have faced a lot worse."

He looked at her for a moment, then said, "Yes, you have, and you are surviving very well. Thank you."

She kissed his palm as he pulled his hand from her cheek. She watched him carry the load of furs into the storefront. The people seemed to congregate on the boardwalk. Willa took a deep breath. She'd had their rude behavior about all she could tolerate. But then this man walked up and started shoving the people around and away from her.

"Go on now, get away all of you. Such shameful behavior."

When they finally cleared out, he turned to face her. "I am very sorry, Mrs. Masterson. I am glad to see you up and about."

"And you, sir, what is your name?"

"I am the reverend, Mildred's father."

His announcement took her back a bit. "I am glad to meet you, sir."

She saw him take in her arm and the sling. "It doesn't work very good anymore. The bullet killed the feeling in my arm to my hand."

"How is the child?"

"The child is fine."

Calvin came out of the store and wanted to charge at the man talking to Willa. She'd finally got over the nightmares, and now he would probably bring it all back.

He got up on the wagon seat and took hold of the reins. "We have a lot to get done."

The reverend tipped his hat and moved away.

Willa put her hand on the post as Calvin moved the wagon out.

"Willa, I need to go to the pig farm to get the pig. The farmer might also have some lambs."

"Then we need to go there first."

"I could leave you at the store if you would like?"

She looked at him. "No, I would rather stay with you, Calvin."

He reached over and grabbed her knee. "I would like that, Willa."

They rode through town. She was glad that Calvin knew where he was going. She saw the same people staring at them as they passed, and she wanted to scream at them all. They had no idea what they had been through.

"It is fine, Willa. They are closeminded and simple, and that is being nice."

Willa couldn't help it, she giggled.

· · ❧ · ·

Willa watched in fascination as they loaded the pig and two sheep onto the wagon. The farmer gave her a pair of sheers for the lamb's fleece and a comb. He explained how to use them and why. Willa thanked him and told him it would be a huge help. He felt very proud of himself.

She decided she wouldn't be lying in the back of the wagon. Thankfully, she had the quilt and pillow she brought up front with her behind her legs. Willa waited on the wagon while Calvin went into the store and bought the supplies they needed. She was thrilled when he came out with a huge barrel of flour for her. He said he wanted lots of bread, and she laughed.

The stupid people still watched her, and she didn't care. Like Calvin said, "closeminded and simple." Calvin heard her and huffed. When he got back into the seat, his hand covered her knee and squeezed it. "Are you ready to go home?"

"So, very ready, Calvin." She watched as he reached into his jacket and pulled out a kitten to give to her. Willa gasped, and the tears flowed down her cheeks. "You remembered."

He leaned to her and kissed her tears away. "I always remember what my love wants." With that, he clicked the reins, and they started home. The kitten fell asleep in her sling.

"How is she doing?"

"She is sleeping. I think it is the wagon rocking."

"I can tell that you would like to join her."

"Oh yes, but I will make it home."

"I will back the wagon up to the barn and unload the animals. The pig will go into one of the stalls. The farmer said after a day or so that the lambs would be fine to roam around the yard and go into the barn at night."

"That sounds good. I don't want anything eating them. We might have to fence the garden to keep them out."

Calvin laughed. "No, we don't want that. The female is pregnant and should have her baby before winter."

"Really? Wow, how good is that."

"I thought I would drive by the fields so you can see how much they have grown."

"I would love to do that, Calvin."

Calvin drove the wagon right up to the fields. When he pulled the wagon to a halt, Willa stood up to see it all. "My goodness, it is so beautiful and green, Calvin. Boy, it all grew and so fast."

"Yes, it looks like we will have a good harvest."

"I can see we will. My arm is getting stronger, so I can help with the harvest."

"I put a notice up to hire some men for the harvest. I have enough funds left, but you can cook for us."

"I will be glad to. You might want to smoke some more rabbits." She laughed at the look he gave her. "Working men need food."

"Rabbits coming up."

"And cornbread, nice combination, and filling."

"Yes, that will work. Maybe even an apple pie or two?"

"Sure, I can do that."

"Your hand is getting better."

"It really is. I have feelings in my arm and hand now. I didn't have that before, Calvin."

"I know, and I saw that you tied the knots."

"I did, all of them."

"What about the kitten? Does it stay in the house or barn?"

"I think it should be in the barn, that way it can keep the mice out of the corn and hay."

"Okay, we will setup a little sleeping area for her."

"I don't want to feed her too much. I want her to hunt for food. A little milk will be good for her. She is still tiny. She will probably mate with a bobcat, and we will have lots of feral cats to control the mice."

"Good idea."

"Ohhh..."

"Willa?"

"It is the baby, Calvin. I think he has decided to come."

"Ohhh."

"Yes, my water just broke, Calvin."

"We should be home in about twenty minutes. Do you think you can last that long?"

She laughed, "I have no idea, Calvin." Willa gripped the post over the contraction that overwhelmed her. She tried to start breathing in short gasps. "Jacob, listen to your mother. You need to hold off for a little while. We need to get home."

Calvin huffed over her order.

"He'll listen, won't you sweet boy?" She smiled at Calvin in between her puffs. "How far, Calvin?" She called out to him during another contraction.

"They are coming rather fast, Jacob." Calvin reached over and placed his hand over the hard ball of baby. "Daddy says you need to slow down a little, big boy."

"I love the outside, Calvin. Guess we can have our baby out here." Willa laughed through the next contraction. "His middle name should be Fields, yup, Fields."

"Okay, Willa, Fields it is. But let's try to get home."

"Good idea. Jacob Fields Masterson, now that is a good, strong name, Calvin."

Right now, Calvin knew he would agree to just about anything she wanted. He would get her inside first, and they would take care of the baby coming. The animals would have to wait a bit.

His guts twisted over the yell that came out of Willa on the next contraction. "I don't think we need another one for a while, Willa." He huffed over the look she tossed him.

"Oh, I don't know. We should have a girl or at least another boy so Jacob has a brother."

Calvin pulled the wagon up to the steps and jumped down. He wished she were stronger for all this. He went around the wagon and lifted Willa out of the seat. "Hang on Willa, I'll have you in bed in just a minute. Her body went stiff in his arms over another contraction.

"I want to push, Calvin. I can feel Jacob moving through me. Wow, it is a marvelous feeling, Calvin.

You better throw the old quilt down."

"Okay, Willa."

Calvin grabbed the quilt she laid out as he walked with her to the bed.

"I have everything ready, Calvin. We best get the stove heated up."

His lips brushed her brow, and he smiled. "Here we go, Willa." He put her into the bed. Calvin pulled her shoes off and her pants as her knees went up. Her hands wrapped around the bedpost over another contraction.

The kitten's head popped out of the sling, and Calvin laughed. He pulled the little bundle of fur out of the sling and set her on the floor. He saw her run under the bed. "Good place to go."

"What is Calvin?"

"Oh, the kitten she ran under the bed."

"Oh, my, maybe she will be a house kitty." She screamed out, "I have to push, Calvin."

Calvin readied himself to catch his son. "Okay, Willa, push away!"

She groaned, and her face crunched up over the effort. "I can see his head, Willa!"

She screamed and pushed harder. "Come on, Jacob, you can come now."

Calvin watched as the baby moved out of her. He'd never seen anything so beautiful. "He is coming, Willa."

"Good thing, I am about done in, Calvin."

"I can imagine."

Calvin's large hand came under the child as it slid out of her. Calvin cut the cord and wrapped the boy in the sheet Willa had ready for him and placed the baby in her waiting arms. The boy's cry filled the room, and Calvin finally breathed. He waited for the afterbirth to come and was relieved when it finally left her. He wrapped up the mess and took it to the door, placing it on the chair on the porch. He would bury it later. He went back to the bed where Willa was cleaning the baby.

"He is so beautiful, Calvin. So, perfect right down to his toes." She pulled the blanket back so Calvin could see his son.

Calvin gathered the small bundle up in arms and marveled at the birth and the woman who had given him this miracle. "Jacob Fields Masterson, a good name."

The boy took hold of his finger, and Calvin smiled. "Isn't he something."

"He is a wonderful gift, Calvin."

He smiled at her. "Yes, he is."

"I'd best feed him before I fall asleep."

He moved the boy back into her arms, and she guided the little guy to her breast. "He is hungry, Calvin." They both watched as the baby drank from her.

"Let me get the bassinet over here for him."

Calvin went over and picked up the small rocking crib for his son. Willa had it all ready for him. He looked over at her, holding his son, and tears rolled down his cheeks. "A very good mother."

Willa finally fell asleep. Calvin walked around the room with his son in his arms. It seemed as if the boy wanted to see everything all at once, and Calvin laughed over the thought. It took a while for the boy to fall asleep. The little boy's eyes slowly closed as he lay in his arms. "I am going to put you down, Jacob, and get the animals taken care of."

He carefully placed the boy in the bassinet within Willa's reach. He watched as her good hand automatically came out to cover the boy's back and pat him to calm him down. He smiled and shook his head, thanking God once again for the gift he had sent him.

To his surprise, the kitten came out from under the bed and crawled into the bassinet at the boy's feet. The kitten's paw went over the baby's legs as she wrapped her body around his little feet. "I guess you are a house kitty and my son's guardian."

With that said, Calvin headed out the door to take care of the animals and bring in the supplies. "It is a beautiful day, as Willa would say."

CHAPTER THIRTEEN

Willa moved and pulled the blanket up Jacob's backside. She reached over and petted the kitten. "Maddy sounds like a good name for you. I guess you have adopted Jacob. House kitty, so be it."

"Yes, she has, Willa."

She looked up and smiled at Calvin. "I think Jacob is worn out."

"Like his mother?"

"Yes, that I am, but in such a good way, Calvin."

"I did get the animals put up and brought in the supplies we got."

"Oh good." She looked over at the stack by the kitchen. "We certainly had a huge day."

"A very good day, Willa."

She saw the bible on the table beside Calvin.

He smiled, "Jacob Fields Masterson is officially recorded in our bible."

"Oh, good. That makes me feel wonderful."

"He is a big boy, Willa."

"Yes, he must be at least six or seven pounds."

"I'd say he is about seventeen inches in length. He will be tall."

"Takes after his father, Calvin."

"He has your eyes, Willa."

"My goodness."

All the while she talked to him her hand moved gently down the baby's back in soothing strokes.

"Would you like something to eat?"

"Maybe later."

The knock on the door made her gasp. "Calvin?"

He raised his hand, "It will be fine, Willa." She saw the gun in his hand resting behind the door as he opened it. "Reverend?"

"May I come in, Calvin?"

"Why are you here, Reverend?"

Willa bit at her lip. Calvin stood before the man in the door.

"I thought I would come by and speak to you about baptizing your son, Calvin." He tipped his hat to her, "Mrs. Masterson."

Calvin looked over to her, and Willa gave him a slight nod.

He stepped back and let the man enter their house. The man's gaze went right to the baby. "Oh my, he is born. Is everything alright?"

Calvin spoke up, "Yes, he is fine. His name is Jacob Fields Masterson."

"That is a proud name, Calvin."

The man walked over and looked at the baby. Tears ran down his cheeks. "He is a big boy."

Willa looked at the man and smiled. "He is healthy, Reverend."

She could visibly see the man relax.

Calvin came to stand by her and his son.

The man finally pulled his attention away from the baby and looked at the two of them. "I know you said you would not be back to church, but I thought I could come out here to baptize the child."

Calvin reached down and took hold of Willa's hand. She squeezed his hand and smiled at him. "We would like that, Reverend."

"I can do it now if you both like?"

Willa said, "I think that would be fine." She looked at Calvin, who nodded in agreement.

Calvin picked up Jacob and placed him in the Reverend's arms.

The man smiled at Jacob and began the baptism. When he finished blessing the child, he placed Jacob in Willa's arms. "He is a wonderful child."

She took Jacob and smiled at the man. "Yes, he is a precious gift from God."

Calvin walked with the Reverend outside.

Willa began feeding Jacob.

Calvin came back in, walked over, and sat beside her. "Jacob is hungry, Willa."

"He is. I will eat dinner. What would you like me to make?"

"I thought I would cook tonight, Willa."

"That sounds good, Calvin."

"How do omelets sound?"

"Yummy. There is also a fresh loaf of bread."

"Would you like some grits?"

"I am sure I will eat some. I am feeding Jacob now, so I must keep my strength up."

Calvin took the boy from her arms and burped him. "That sounded bigger than he is, Willa."

They both laughed.

"Thank you, Willa. The man needed to do that."

"I know, Calvin. I am also glad Jacob is baptized."

CHAPTER FOURTEEN

"Oh my gosh, Calvin, look at the cat." They stared and then laughed over the cat holding on to Jacob's shirt to keep him on the blanket. "She definitely treats him like her kitten."

"He has gotten so big, Willa."

"Oh, I know. He is growing fast."

She looked over at Calvin and smiled at the way he studied her.

"You want to tell me something, Willa?"

"I think you can guess, Calvin."

He huffed at her. "This one will be a girl."

"A girl? Really?"

"Yes, you are carrying her higher than you did, Jacob."

He came over and kneeled before her and then put his head on her stomach. She heard him talk to the baby as her fingers stroked his hair. "I think she will come after winter, Calvin."

"Winter or spring, we will love her."

Dinner was ready. Willa thought she might need to go in and baste the roast. They were waiting on the Reverend. He seemed to be a regular visitor and always on Saturday. Willa knew he felt more comfortable out here at the farm. She felt he didn't like town much, though he never said anything. She and Calvin discussed it and decided he was welcome to move out here. Calvin even started building a small cabin for the man. It wasn't much, but like Calvin said, if the man didn't use it, one of the kids could.

She looked at her husband and knew he was concerned that the man had not shown up. He was usually very prompt on time. Calvin began pacing across the porch. "He is late, Calvin."

"Yes, it is not like him."

"I need to feed Jacob and get him down for the night. I think..."

He came over, and his lips pressed into her brow. "That I should go find him?"

She smiled at him. "Yes, I think you better."

Calvin walked over and picked up Jacob, who started laughing when Calvin blew on his tummy.

Willa followed them into the house.

"Please lock the door, Willa. And you have your gun?"

"Yes, on both counts, Calvin."

She hoped the man was okay. "Okay, my little love, you must be hungry." Calvin left to get the horse, and Willa set Jacob in his chair and dished up some roast and vegetables for him. The boy was a good eater.

She heard the horse leaving the yard and went to the window to watch Calvin leave. "Stay safe, my love."

Willa automatically locked the door, then reached down and touched the gun at her hip. She started carrying it in her pocket all the time since the shooting.

. . ᪥ . .

Willa moved away from Jacob's crib. The boy finally fell asleep. "He must have felt my nervousness."

She walked over to the window again and looked out. It was too dark to see anything, but she tried. She felt Calvin had been gone long enough to reach town, but she didn't think he would go there. After the way the people acted when they went into town, neither of them wanted anything to do with them. She honestly felt the Reverend was disappointed in the people as well, though he wouldn't say anything.

Just as she turned to leave the window, she heard the hoofbeats. "Calvin..."

Willa swung the door open and watched Calvin tie his horse off and walk around to the Reverend's.

"I found him on the ground, Willa. He is passed out, and I don't know what is wrong."

"We best put him in front of the fireplace, Calvin, for the heat and light."

She rushed back into the house and spread the old quilt before the fire. She threw another log onto the fire. Calvin laid the man out on the quilt.

"I am going to put the horses up in the barn, Willa."

"Alright, Calvin. I will try and make him comfortable."

"I will be back to help you with his clothes."

"Yes." Willa managed to get the man's boots off. She checked him over and couldn't find any blood on his clothes. Willa did see a big, dark bump on his forehead. She needed to wait for Calvin to do the rest. She didn't have the strength in her hands to do it.

She heard Calvin come in. "I didn't see any blood, Calvin." When he didn't answer, she looked over and stared into the barrel of a long gun. She looked up and into the angry eyes of a man she didn't know.

"There won't be any blood. He fell off the horse when it reared."

Her mouth opened, and then she snapped it shut.

"I wouldn't mind some of that meal, I smell."

She nodded in silence, unsure what to do, but feed him. As she pushed to her feet, she looked at the door.

"He won't be coming in. I tied him up in the barn."

Willa's knees went weak over what the man said he did, but she knew it could be worse. She felt relief. She didn't hear any shots, Calvin was alive, and that is what counted.

She moved into the kitchen and started fixing a plate for the man. She set it on the table with silverware and a glass of milk. Willa could feel him watching every move she made. She heard Jacob stir and started walking over to the crib. She saw the man jump and then settle down, and he took his seat at the table.

"How old is he?"

"About six months."

"You are the one that man's daughter shot."

There was no sense in avoiding the man or his conclusions. "Yes, I am."

The stranger never took his gaze away from her. "You are having another one."

It wasn't a question; her hand automatically moved to cover the beginning of the first sign of the baby. "I am. She should come at the end of winter."

The man huffed, and Willa swallowed down the tears that wanted to flow.

"That bitch daughter of his took my Cecily's life."

Willa gasped over the man's outburst. "I am so sorry."

"You killed her, didn't you?"

"Yes, it was either that or get shot again."

He nodded as if he understood. Willa had a feeling he did.

"I still can't use my hand or arm that well. I do have some feelings coming back." She wasn't sure why she told him that.

"It might never come back all the way."

"No, probably not, but at least I can feel it now."

"Why do you let that man into your house?"

Willa looked over at the Reverend and then off in thought. "I've asked myself that many times. But he isn't his daughter. She was the evil one, not him."

She refused to look at him, not really caring what he thought.

His fork hit the plate, and Willa looked over at him. "Would you like some more?"

"No, it was very good, Mrs. Masterson."

She stared at him for a moment and decided, "Who are you?"

"I am George Grooper."

"We stopped going to church in town after what happened. We didn't know that she hurt any other people. She was crazy, and those people in town are small-minded, as my husband says."

Mr. Grooper huffed in amusement over her comment.

"Your husband will be fine, Mrs. Masterson. He will have a headache but nothing else. I didn't come here to harm any of you. I only want the man in front of your fireplace."

She looked at him, "Killing him won't change anything, Mr. Grooper."

"No, probably not, but it will feel good knowing he is gone."

"But what about you? How will you deal with doing it? You will have to live with it every day. I know you lost your love. I can see that all over you. Don't do something that will ruin the memories the two of you created.

You see if I lost Calvin, I don't think I could go on." He didn't answer her. "I still have nightmares over killing Mildred, even knowing I had no choice. But Calvin is my world. That day, all I could think of was Calvin and the child we created, a baby from our love. He is what counted at that moment, only him."

Calvin rolled his head against the door as the tears trailed down his cheeks. Busting through the door was all he wanted to do until he heard her talking to George. Calvin cried over the man's loss; he didn't know Mildred killed his wife. Now, to hear what Willa told the man made the heartbreak over George's loss even worse.

It seemed like forever, but Calvin felt it was only minutes. George came plowing through the door, heading to the barn. The man stopped and turned to look at Calvin. "Be thankful, very blessed, Calvin, that you still have her."

With that, the man went to the barn and then rode out. Calvin had a feeling they would never see George again.

Calvin turned to race into the house and straight to Willa, who stood there crying. "Oh, my dear, sweet girl." He pulled her into his arms and hugged her to him. She held onto him as if she could erase all the bad in the world by holding him. "He is gone, Willa."

"The poor man lost everything, Calvin. He lost it all."

He pulled her closer, letting her sob against his chest. His hand ran down her hair, and he knew how blessed he was with Willa.

The Reverend closed his eyes to give the couple the time they needed. He knew the lady just saved his life and that of George Grooper.

CHAPTER FIFTEEN

The reverend passed Calvin another board. "You sure she is only carrying one baby?"

They both turned and looked at Willa, who was hanging up clothes on the line.

"I think it is just one. I agree she is getting bigger than when she carried Jacob."

"We will see soon enough."

Calvin snicker over the man's matter of fact announcement. He wondered how this man became part of their family. The cabin was almost finished, and he would move in once it was done.

The Reverend, or Tom as he wanted to be called now, did decide to move to the farm. He gave up the church and told Calvin it was never right since Mildred. They never really spoke about his daughter. It was a subject both he and Willa decided would be left buried in the past.

Calvin watched Willa lift her arm to pin the blouse to the line. It was a slow but very determined process for Willa. He smiled, knowing how stubborn his wife could be. That she accepted Tom's presence in their lives still amazed him.

He thought back over George. They never did see him again. The man left town and never returned after the incident. Calvin hoped he found a new life.

When he thought about it, having Tom here did help him with the farm. They harvested the corn and cut the oat stocks that were drying in the field. Tomorrow, they would go and begin gathering the hay. The men he hired would be back early in the morning.

Calvin looked over at the lambs and huffed. They were sheered with Tom's help. Willa had her fleece and already spun many shanks of yarn. It was a lot of work for her, but she loved it. She even tried dying a few shanks with blackberries and some blueberries she gathered. She wished she'd found strawberries. Maybe next year, he could plant some for her.

He hammered the last nail into the roof beam. "There, that finishes it."

Calvin watched as Tom stepped back and took in the erected cabin. "It is really wonderful, Calvin."

"Tomorrow, we will finish the chimney and the shelving inside, and you will have your home."

"Just wonderful."

Calvin turned away to give time to the man and his emotions. "I am going to check on Willa, Tom."

"Yes, you best do that. I saw her holding her back. A sure sign the baby is near to coming."

Calvin laughed as he left the man to find Willa. He headed to the barn figuring she went there to care for the animals. "She does love her animals."

He saw the kittens run under the barn and laughed. As she said, they now had many cats and no mice. "And that is a good thing." He watched as Jacob ran around trying to catch a kitten. "He needs more practice running." He waved to his son and smiled as the boy ran to him. "Hi there, Jacob. Where is Mommy?"

"Singing to the cow, Daddy."

He lifted Jacob in his arms and settled him on his shoulders. "I think your sister is going to be here with us and soon." The boy clapped.

"Mary will be pretty, Daddy."

"Mary, is it?"

"Yes, Mommy told me we needed a good name for her. I like Mary."

"It is a pretty name, Jacob."

"Mommy said I picked the per...?"

"Perfect."

"Yes, that."

"I agree, Jacob."

Jacob leaned forward and whispered into Calvin's ear. "If it is a brother, Joseph will be good."

Calvin whispered back. "I think you are right. What about a middle name, like yours is Fields."

Jacob whispered back as they walked into the barn. "Berry, Daddy."

"That will be a wonderful name, Jacob. What about Mary's middle name?"

"Mommy picked that, Daddy."

"She did?"

"Oh yes, Blossom. That will be Mary's other name."

"I like that one too, Jacob."

Calvin closed his eyes for a moment and breathed in his wonderful life. "Special, she is so special."

"Who, Daddy?"

"Your Mommy, Jacob."

The boy giggled and said. "I know that, Daddy." And they both laughed.

"And what are my boys all happy about?"

Calvin lifted Jacob down. The boy took off after the baby lamb. For his age, he was big.

Willa smiled over the far-off look Calvin took as his attention followed his son.

"He grew again, Calvin. It is a good thing I know how to sew."

He swung about and gathered her to him, then spun her about. "You, my love, are beautiful."

Her hands squeezed his shoulders. "That is because I love this wonderful man."

Willa's laughter echoed off the walls of the barn.

"So, how is our daughter doing?"

She kissed him before answering. "I think she is getting ready to come to us."

"That, my love, will be marvelous."

Willa hugged him. "The cabin looks finished."

He smiled at her. "Almost. We still need to get the chimney finished."

"Make sure to put an oven in the side of it for him."

"Already planned out."

"Good. I think he will like his independence. He already asked me for the cornbread recipe. I've written a sheet of the various recipes he likes so he can make them for himself."

Calvin kissed the side of her neck and started back up to her ear.

She moaned, "Dear husband, I will be very glad when our daughter comes."

"Mary will be here soon."

She giggled into his shoulder, and Calvin groaned.

"Now, I know what you two were discussing."

"Yes, and I was also informed of his brother's name should he arrive in place of Mary."

"It will always be a surprise. I thought Jacob should be aware of that fact."

"Glad you thought of it. Now, he will accept what comes."

"And so will we."

. . ⁓ . .

The End

Did you love *Willa's Love*? Then you should read *Do You Believe in Magic?*[1] by Jewel Adams!

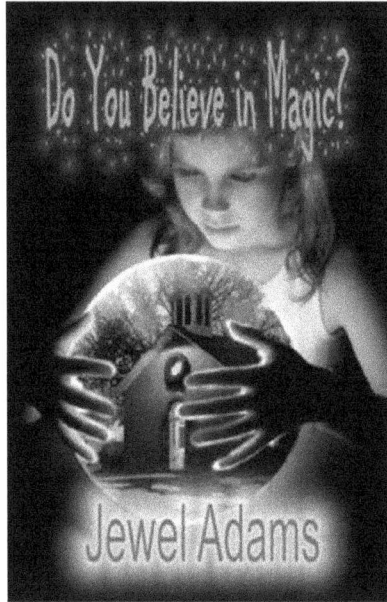

Do You Believe in Magic?The flash of shiny metal caught his attention just in time to move as the bullet whizzed past his head. "Hey! Inside! I'm Captain Clay Banyon of the US Army, put the damn gun away!" He took a deep breath to control his temper. "The Indians are gone, you can come out now."Ali's only problem was she didn't want to come out or even be here! Just seeing anything beyond the stagecoach might be more than her mind could handle.When Ali gave in and played her goddaughter's game pretending they live in the old west, using a garage sale, glass-ball relic, little did she know—magic would change their lives forever.She possessed a name, a profession and felt ridiculously grateful to the power that brought them to this...magic time.

Read more at https://books2read.com/ap/Rwd3Xd/Jewel-Adams.

1. https://books2read.com/u/4NydkW

2. https://books2read.com/u/4NydkW

About the Author

Jewel AdJewel Adams - Best Selling Author of Romance with a Touch of Spice!Hi, I am Jewel Adams an author of various romance genres I love to write an adventure in my story and fell in love with Time Travel Romances. I currently have ten stand alone novels in my Loves in Time series. Yes, these books can be read in any order, only two are sequels Answers In Time that follows Gamble in Time, and Nick's Redemption In Time that follows Dream Lover.Don't forget to check out my new Fantasy series Internal Heritage. The fourth book in the series just came out :) They are all very exciting reads, enjoy.I also have an Amish Romance series that includes five books, these do follow each other and all contain the same characters. My friend Bev Haynes and I write the Quilted Hill series together.My All Time Best Seller - SAVAGE DESTINY a white captive Indian story that takes place during the early western movement in America. This love story will stay in your heart forever.We can never forget DO YOU BELIEVE IN MAGIC a sweet Romance Time Travel set in the west. This and Savage Destiny are my favorite covers of all time. My friend Bev Haynes is a true cover artist. All the covers you see are done by Bev Haynes.I just released the tenth novel in the Loves In Time-Romance Time Travel series IMPOSTOR IN TIME. Erin discovers when the nightmare becomes reality the adventure begins. Life is hardly the same where Erin finds herself, it is hard and paved with danger. Erin has to hold on to the love she discovers and face her new reality or be swallowed by the evil that stalks her.Always check back to see what I am up to :) JewelJewel Adamshttps://books2read.com/ap/Rwd3Xd/Jewel-AdamsRomance with a Touch of SpiceLook for new and spicy releases...ams

Read more at https://books2read.com/ap/Rwd3Xd/Jewel-Adams.

Milton Keynes UK
Ingram Content Group UK Ltd.
UKHW030143051224
452010UK00001B/195